THE *Exile*
& THE SACRED TRAVELLERS

ALSO BY MARIE-CLAIRE BLAIS

Fiction

The Angel of Solitude
Anna's World
David Sterne
Deaf to the City
The Fugitive
A Literary Affair
Mad Shadows
The Manuscripts of Pauline Archange
Nights in the Underground
A Season in the Life of Emmanuel
Tête Blanche
These Festive Nights
The Wolf

Nonfiction

American Notebooks: A Writer's Journey

Drama

Wintersleep

THE *Exile*
& THE SACRED TRAVELLERS

Marie-Claire Blais

Translated by
NIGEL SPENCER

Introduction by
RONALD B. HATCH

RONSDALE PRESS

The Exile & The Sacred Travellers was originally published by Bibliothèque québécoise as *L'exilé: nouvelles; suivi de, Les voyageurs sacrés* (1992).

RONSDALE PRESS
3350 West 21st Avenue
Vancouver, B.C., Canada
V6S 1G7

Set in New Baskerville: 11 pt on 15
Typesetting: Julie Cochrane
Printing: Hignell Printing, Winnipeg, Manitoba
Cover Art: Susan Madsen, detail of "The Persistent Ones" (1997),
    oil on canvas, 36" x 36". Photo credit: Stephen D. Mitchell
Cover Design: Julie Cochrane

Ronsdale Press wishes to thank the Canada Council for the Arts, the Government of Canada through the Book Publishing Industry Development Program (BPIDP), and the Province of British Columbia through the British Columbia Arts Council for their support of its publishing program.

CANADIAN CATALOGUING IN PUBLICATION DATA

Blais, Marie-Claire, 1939–
   [Exilé. English]
   The exile, &, The sacred travellers

Translation of: L'exilé: nouvelles; suivi de, Les voyageurs sacrés.
ISBN 0-921870-79-5

1. Spencer, Nigel, 1945– II. Blais, Marie-Claire, 1939– Voyageurs sacrés. English.
III. Title. IV. Title: Sacred travellers.
PS8503.L33E8613 2000   C843'.54   C00-910547-6
PQ3919.B6E9213 2000

Contents

—◦◦◦—

Marie-Claire Blais and the Art of Short Fiction

An Introduction

EVER SINCE THE PUBLICATION of her first novel, *La belle bête,* in 1959 (*Mad Shadows,* 1960), Marie-Claire Blais has been a dominant presence on the Québec literary scene, with the publication almost every year of a novel, or collection of poems, or a play. She has received many prizes both in France and Canada, including three Governor General's awards, most recently for *These Festive Nights* (1997). Blais is, however, less well known for her short fiction, and it is hoped that the publication of *The Exile & The Sacred Travellers,* translated by Nigel Spencer from the original edition — *L'exilé: nouvelles; suivi de, Les voyageurs sacrés* (1992) — will allow readers to enjoy her great artistry in this subtlest and most demanding of all narrative forms. The collection comprises nine short stories and a novella, "The Sacred Travellers." With the exception of the novella, which appears last although published first, the stories are arranged chronologically by their publication date and offer an overview of Blais' fiction for more than 25 years — from 1962 to 1989.

Blais is renowned for her experiments in rendering complex

states of mind with experimental narrative styles, and certainly this collection contains a wide range of different kinds of story. One finds bold, brightly coloured portraits of rural Québec, with collo-quial Québécois dialogue, as well as meditative psychological por-traits, and stories that are almost poems as they develop through a sinuous lyrical style, with Blais' trademark long sentences and even longer paragraphs which circle back on themselves to evoke the many contradictions of conscious and unconscious experience.

An unusual feature of Blais' fiction is what one might call its oth-erworldly quality, its lack of a precise setting. It is certainly possible to ascribe locales to many of the stories. For example, Judith in "The New School Mistress" speaks of the village being in the north, and her accent would indicate she is from rural Québec. Similarly, "The Exile" is set on a southern island which may well be Key West, where Blais spends part of each year. Yet these are guesses, for Blais rarely specifies a setting, and this fact contributes to a fable-like quality which pervades much of her fiction. Or perhaps it is fairer to say that the lack of precise setting gives Blais' fiction a meta-physical dimension, a characteristic that has much in common with the effect of Samuel Beckett's plays and novels. As she says of one of her characters in "Torment," he moves "between sky and sea," and this primeval backdrop strips away the surface clutter of so much realistic fiction to lay bare the existential journey from birth to death which each person must take, and which so often seems filled with compromise and defined by the measure of mate-rial success. Blais has often been described as a writer of darkness whose characters find little joy in their lives. While this is in part true, it is because she focuses on moments that bring out the des-perate quality of the struggle for form and meaning in human life. She does not describe suffering for the sake of suffering, but to elicit the costs associated with strategies for what society common-ly calls successful living.

It has sometimes been suggested that Blais, as a Québec writer, creates characters who express the sense of loss of self that the people of Québec inherited as a result of the abandonment of the colony by France. The critic Philip Stratford in his short study, *Marie-Claire Blais* (Toronto, Forum House, 1971), has gone so far as to declare that her characters belong to "the generation of death" in Québec. While there may be some truth to these descriptions of her work, they miss the fact that in both her life and her writing Blais has an international reach. Her characters in these stories are widely divergent; there are not only Québécois, but Black Americans, civil rights activists, and artists living in the culture capitals of Europe, to name only a few. Blais' fiction also displays transfiguring compassion for people who are often forgotten, forgotten especially by cultural historians who delineate the dominant trends of a particular time and place. Perhaps because Blais herself grew up in a poor family and left school early to work in a shoe factory, she has always had great sympathy for the plight of individuals cast aside, those left behind by the march of history. In choosing to focus on apparently hopeless characters and situations, Blais reaches down to the essential core of her people to depict their lives, not just in terms of what appears to be the locally significant, but against the inevitable arc of mortality. Her stories, which appear at first to be involved only with the quotidian, open up to a timeless scale — and it is this sudden enlargement that gives her work such power and resonance.

The collection's opening story, "The New School Mistress," was first published as "La nouvelle institutrice" in a special Canadian edition of *Les Lettres nouvelles* (Paris, December 1966–January 1967), and reminds one of the style and subject matter of Blais' most famous early novel, *A Season in the Life of Emmanuel* (1965). At the time of writing "The New School Mistress," Blais had thought it would be part of a sequel to that novel, which she planned to entitle *Testament de Jean-Le Maigre à ses frères,* but the novel never appeared and the story now exists on its own. "The New School Mistress" explodes with energy, especially in the title character of the new school mistress, Judith Prunelle. For the first time, Blais allows a character to speak with a strong regional Québec accent, which makes for vigorous dialogue. It should be added that such an accent also presents a challenge to any translator.

"The New School Mistress" offers a dark picture of rural Québec, typical of those that many Québec writers created after the Quiet Revolution of the early 1960s. These writers chose to depict early twentieth-century Québec as the "Grande Noirceur," the great darkness, perhaps partly in rebellion against the many earlier writers who romanticized the rural life of the habitant on the land, the *terroir*. Yet it would be wrong to read the story entirely in realistic or naturalistic terms as a description of desolation, since Blais, through her strong, graphic style, reminiscent of a woodblock print, gives tremendous vitality to the new school mistress and the children. The story inhabits a territory that combines the gothic with the naive, which gives it immense energy in spite of the backwardness of the village. In part this is because the characters themselves are invested with mythical qualities. Judith Prunelle arrives on the scene, "Fresh out of heaven, of course, in a cloud of dust that still covered her from head to toe, and dragging behind her all the saints she could name." The English reader cannot help hearing an echo of Wordsworth at this point, but Blais' description contains, of course, a delightful irony that distances her from the Romantics.

In the encounter between the new school mistress, with all her energy, and the priest whom we first meet "pulling his bicycle out of a bog," Blais might appear to be describing the struggle between the developing new secularism and the older religious sensibility. While there is something of this social struggle in the story, it quickly becomes clear that the new school mistress, with all her distrust of the priesthood, has little that she can offer the children besides a listing of the Kings of France. Moreover, it turns out that her favourite story to tell the children is the "Creation of the World," drawn directly from the Old Testament. As the story progresses it becomes evident that both the new school mistress and the priest are part of the dysfunctionality of the community and, as is so often the case in Blais' fiction, we are caused to turn our attention away from the "leaders" to the people themselves.

What stands out in the end in "The New School Mistress" is the children. Josephine, one of Judith's students, is convinced that she has had visions of Our Lady, who has come several times to her to reveal important truths. And certainly Josephine is described as someone mystically naive. Whereas the new school mistress's stories of the creation are filled with awe-inspiring scenes of violent origins, Josephine has secret messages from Our Lady teaching compassion and peace. Yet this mysticism cannot be taken at face value, for the story suggests that it, too, is a manifestation of the dysfunctional social dynamic in the community, a dynamic that is made all the more powerful in the surprise ending which couples violence with simplicity and offers a sudden, new entreé to the mysterious world of children.

Following "The New School Mistress" is "Act of Pity" (published as "Un acte de pitié" in *Douze écrivains, douze nouvelles*, Liberté-Ici Radio-Canada, March–April, 1969). While the setting of "Act of Pity" would appear to be similar to that of "The New School Mistress," the story is different in feeling and tone: a psychological study of a priest who has won the esteem and devotion of his parishioners, but who inwardly knows that he has not been able to connect with these people. The priest has set himself off from his fellow human beings, ironically in the "Vallée d'Or," and cannot feel genuine pity for his people because he cannot accept their condition — their poverty and their tortured sense of *amour-propre*. He has become a creature devoted to God and not to humanity, and as such has nurtured a false sense of pride. Not unexpectedly, the priest comes to the realization of his sterility when asked to give the last rites to a young girl, named Maria, and believes that she has seen through him. Although the priest has given himself to God and forsworn the happiness of this world, he has never been able to accept the world as it is, living apart in his own spiritual isolation, wanting to believe that he at least is redeemed through God's justice. The parable-like quality of the story is evident, and gives the thoughtful reader a clear direction for the following stories, in which Blais confronts us with what she sees as a generalized temptation for people to turn away from the actual conditions of mortality to live in intellectual constructs.

Certainly this temptation is evident in "Dispossession" (published as "Dépossession" in *Possibles,* Montréal, vol 10, no 1, Autumn 1985), where Blais takes up the theme of the downtrodden, but now presents it from the point of view of the urban desolate who is dying alone in a crowd of people — from hunger and illness. He is waiting for help from his fellow human beings, help that he has convinced himself will come — for how can it not in a civilized country imbued with humanitarian ideals? Yet even as he waits, with all his ideals intact, we realize that he is succumbing to his condition and that the end of the story marks the end of his life.

"Tenderness" first appeared as "Tendresse" in *Brèves* (Villelongue d'Aude, no. 25–26, Spring 1987), and is one of the most hauntingly beautiful of the stories in this collection, combining both great love and sadness. It tells of two women who have met "just hours before" and are now waking after lovemaking. "Tenderness" is a mood piece which evokes the bitter-sweet sense of closeness that the two women experience — a closeness possible only because they are soon to part. The story captures the surprise the women feel in their connectedness, in being in an oasis "neither had ever been to before." They appear to have lived in isolation, going about their lives doing the things that are felt to be necessary, but here in this space there is a sense of being-at-oneness, all the more powerful because they can drink the "salt tears" that come from lives lived essentially alone.

"Revolutionary and Friend," which was first published as "L'amie révolutionnaire" (*Depuis 25 ans,* Les Presses Laurentiennes, 1987), appears at first to depict the exact opposite of the many Blais characters who are lost and unconnected. It tells the story of a remarkable young woman who has given up her life to revolutionary causes and who feels secure in her decisions. Yet as the plot unfolds and the narrator recounts her friend's many actions in various civil rights conflicts, the story itself begins to evoke a curious sense of distance, of alienation, for it becomes evident that the narrator, who regards the revolutionary as a friend, has never been able to understand this woman. What caused her to give up the life of an artist's contemplation for one of activism is never explained, perhaps cannot be explained. Because the revolutionary's life and her causes are seen entirely from the outside, the woman appears, at least to the narrator — and thus to reader — to be isolated in her very connectedness to others. And Blais' narrative ending, which undercuts the story's apparent closure, elicits an unsettling sense of incompletion.

"The Exile," first published as "L'exilé" (*L'Atelier imaginaire*, Québec, L'Instant même, 1987), is a superb example of Blais' depiction of modern damnation. This time Blais allows her narration to take us inside the mind of her principal character, Christopher, a Black, who has been thrown out of his family home when he spurned his father's choice for him of a career in the military. At the time of the story, he is living in destitute circumstances on a southern tourist island. In his own mind, however, Christopher thinks of himself as a rebel against what he considers the worst excesses of both Black and White America. Strangely, he sees himself rebelling against the ideologies of the United States through his own body, through his own physical beauty. In the past he has been a model in Los Angeles, and even, it is suggested, a male prostitute, but this does not bother him, and indeed he regards his rebellion as an act that combines the physical and the aesthetic, which will allow him to become a part of what he sees as elegant patrician society. On the island he desperately holds himself aloof from the other Blacks who are poor; he wants to live for pleasure, for the "voluptuous lifestyle of the rich." He imagines being able to live out his sensuality without compunction, while the Whites continue to live in fear and guilt. Through Christopher, Blais gives a striking example of what Frantz Fanon described as the colonized taking on the manners of the colonizer. For Christopher, the surface of things has become all important. From his destitute position on the island he glories in the thought that he will become a waiter, for dressed in white he will be able to participate in what he sees as the dance-like elegance of the wealthy. The difference between how Christopher feels within himself and the glimpses we have of the world he inhabits gives an uncanny sense of dislocation, of the extent to which individuals live within their own created selves, struggling to make the world fit their own definitions.

"Voyage" was first published as "Le voyage" in *Voix de pères, voix de filles* (Paris, Maren Sell & Cie, 1988). Where "Exile" gives only hints of the causes of the protagonist's psychic dislocation, "Voyage" offers a much more socio-economic explanation. The story takes as its starting point a young girl who *knows* that she is not real. She knows this because her father repeatedly tells her "that the real people lived far away in strange countries, where they suffered, died, and were sacrificed in wars that bathed the sky in blood." The story is highly suggestive of a colonial situation in which reality exists only at the centre of empire while the colonials exist on the margin in a form of unreality. Indeed, the family of the young girl continually take it upon themselves to explain away their difficult times, the fact that there are rats in their neighbourhood and babies are bitten in their cribs. The father is typical of the hardworking wage earner who takes his lot in life equably. While the mother is angered at the way the bosses treat her husband, she can do nothing to change the situation. The parents of "she-who-wasn't-really-anybody" have even adopted an oriental boy, Kimo, from an orphanage, in an attempt to show that they are in a position to help others. And of course having to look after Kimo serves only to make "she-who-wasn't-really-anybody" feel more unlike the other children around, more unreal. As a recompense for all this unreality, the father promises the young girl that some day they will go and live in the country, that he would no longer "work in the dangerous, smoke-filled plant that robbed men of their health and hopes." The country here represents the pastoral refuge of romanticism in the face of industrialization, and as such must inevitably disappoint. The "real" people always live elsewhere. The question remains of how to become *someone* in a caged world of unreality where the apparent alternative appears to be a hidden mirror image.

"Torment," first published as "Le tourment" (*L'Atelier imaginaire*, Lausanne, L'Âge d'Homme, 1988), resembles "The Exile" in many ways, but carries the theme of exile and damnation one step further. The protagonist, Gentry, is living on a southern tourist island and working as a bartender, slowly but steadily drinking himself into oblivion. The poignancy of the story lies in Gentry's promising beginnings, his idealism. As a young man he had been a medical student at Harvard. Then, at the time of the Vietnam War, he chose to become a conscientious objector, with the result that he was forced to flee the U.S., and has gradually declined to his present lowly condition. Yet there is still something of the old idealism present, a longing for a different kind of world, as can be seen in Gentry's disdain for the rich tourists who have no memory of the war, of the bombings, of the "faces of little girls running through the flames." When the present is placed against the past, everything in the tourist resort seems trivial to Gentry. Worse still, he finds that he must contend with a wounded Vietnam vet who still glories in the torching of Vietnamese villages. But not only does Gentry find the world around him facile and sordid, when he looks into his own past, he finds much that he cannot forgive about himself. Both inside the character and outside there seems to be desolation. What adds an additional twist of the knife is Blais' suggestion that Gentry has not travelled far enough into that desolation, for he is still ill at ease about his decision to combat his own country and endorses, at some level, the very world that he has intellectually fought against. Hell, Gentry discovers, is memory — and memory not as nostalgia, tradition or stoic fortress, but as the insidious enemy within that refuses all passage.

"An Intimate Death" was first published as "Mort intime" (*L'Atelier imaginaire*, Lausanne, L'Âge d'Homme, 1989). The story captures the sudden death of a promising young writer. The cause of death is not given, but AIDS is strongly suggested. Blais' narrative moves back and forth from the time of vitality and parties to the slow dissipation and final end, but the story is constructed so that one is never sure when the end comes. The sense of death in life is very powerfully presented: "a young man died still full of the stuff of life, his books and writing still intact on the shelves and on his table . . . and that night , they celebrated him." The prose captures the way death slowly, almost casually, infiltrates the man, taking him away even as the stream of celebration continues. It is hard to believe that the man, so vitally alive and in love with life, is now dying/dead. In this regard it reminds one of Tolstoy's famous story "The Death of Ivan Ilych," but instead of Tolstoy's rendering of the horror of Ivan's realization that the world will not miss him, Blais develops the experience from inside and outside so life blends into death and death into life with a fluidity that takes all horror from the event and all profundity. It is a chilling depiction of the mundane in its all-conquering intractability.

"The Sacred Travellers" was first published in *Écrits du Canada français* as "Les voyageurs sacrés, ou l'invraisemblable instant" in 1962. It is the longest and most challenging of the pieces in this collection, and was originally subtitled "Poème," which points to its quality of poetic prose. It was first translated into English by Derek Coltman and published in 1967 by Farrar, Straus and Giroux as one of two novellas in the volume *The Day is Dark and Three Travelers*. This was then reissued by Penguin in 1985 under the same title, with an introduction by Janet M. Paterson, but with no indication of Coltman as the translator.

As a novella, one expects "The Sacred Travellers" to develop through a series of moments over a period of time. But Blais repeats this novella structure in two further dimensions. Not only does the story take place in a chronological sequence, beginning on one Sunday and ending on another, but there is a geographical sequence of places, frequently at famous cathedrals. And these sequences are placed within the movements of a musical composition (First Instant, Interlude, Second Instant) with musical notations such as *allegro ma non troppo*. The effect is a seamless blend of time, place and aesthetic form, perfectly suited to the description of the love affair among the three main characters: Montserrat who is a sculptor married to Miguel, a playwright, and Johann, a musician with whom Montserrat falls in love and has an affair which breaks up the relationship — begun in childhood — between Montserrat and Miguel. The translation into English is by no means easy, in part because the French language has two different ways of indicating the speaker, but also because handling the stream of consciousness of three different characters is itself elusive, and there are times when context alone will allow one to discover who is speaking. This is of course Blais' intention: to create a sense of a three-sided love affair in which each of the trio knows the thoughts of the others. The characters are brought together by this knowledge but also pushed apart.

By calling attention to the form of the novella in various dimensions, indeed by overdetermining that form, Blais underlines the manner in which the lovers attempt to live their lives as works of art without actually taking account of the world around them. They spin out into language that, for a time, dominates space and time. It almost seems as though language as art can conquer everyday reality as we know it, creating an *invraisemblable* or improbable moment. This is a major theme for Blais, and nowhere else does she manage to create the shimmering surface of life as art so evocatively. A number of critics have expressed dislike for the work, and certainly it makes great demands upon the reader, but once one enters into the different worlds of the three artists —

sculptor, playwright and musician — their worlds blend into one shimmering delight of words that for a time seems to hold out against the world of mundane existence. As always in Blais, however, the mundane reasserts itself.

The stories in *The Exile & The Sacred Travellers* not only offer a fine introduction to the major themes of Blais' writing, they also show Blais working at the height of her powers in short fiction. Blais here uses the strictures of brief narrative form as an epiphanic means of allowing us to draw close to and yet see round her characters. Her stories both recreate and strip away the cultural and mental forms humanity develops in an attempt to control its destiny and, by so doing, these fictions ultimately open for our felt attention the vastness of eternity which we attempt to call home.

— Ronald B. Hatch
University of British Columbia

The New
School Mistress

"So where's he live, this School Inspector?" Judith Prunelle demanded of Father Philippe Rougement, who at this moment, was pulling his bicycle out of a bog with one hand and shaking his cassock with the other. "Jesus-Mary-Mother-of-God, I'm lost!"

"Not quite so loud, please. I'm not deaf," he replied.

And so it was the new school mistress at l'École du Repentir came to this forlorn village. The absence of a teacher for three years had obliged Father Philippe to make home visits in order to instruct children in their catechism — a fruitless and disappointing exercise, for not a single family had wanted him there, except Grandma Antoinette, and even she, probably ashamed of her poverty and hiding her broken-down house, had only greeted him at the front steps . . . her long, austere shadow barring the way.

"Oh, Dear God, what a teacher you've sent us!" he thought, looking at the young girl standing in the middle of the road with a torn suitcase in her hand, saying in her rough dialect, "Jesus-Mary-and-Joseph, where'm I at?"

Fresh out of heaven, of course, in a cloud of dust that still covered her from head to toe, and dragging along behind her all the saints she could name (St. Chrysostom, St. Luke and St. Paul) and chewing these into a cud with other provocative words, sacred vessels and the like: "By the Holy Cross, I wish I was outta here!" She saw language, rich in colour, only through the prism of blasphemy, for this fishwife's spirit was stirred by a vivid imagination and a rebellion all in incense and gold.

"My child," said the priest, shrugging his shoulders, "I must ask you to watch your language," but she was indifferent to this man, more of a boy really, a playmate she could push around by waving a bony fist in his face. Judith had no experience but of growing up with eight mean, belligerent brothers, and of being happier with lumberjacks than with girls her own age. Proud and disdainful, living isolated, or sometimes hardly living at all, the young girl rarely allowed her insatiable vigour — well hidden by scrappiness — to surface on her wild, adolescent features, as she swore and spat in all directions. Still, this same girl had somehow managed, in some obscure school or other, to obtain the yellowed diploma she now pulled from her pocket, smugly satisfied.

"See, school mistress . . . I toldja. An' I'll talk any way I wanta, bejesus," she said, actually waving the bony fist in his pallid face, and following it with a river of insults: "I don't like priests. They're borin'."

Father Philippe listened in helpless silence, his eyes closed. Her fervent swearing done, Judith now fell silent. After a pause, she asked for the time and also about the Inspector General of Schools. "I'm sorry," he said. "I don't know where he lives. I'm new here, myself. I'm not even sure we have one."

Judith could not imagine her school without an inspector, and she had even been told at home that she should find lodging with him. She showed the priest a letter signed by the mayor of Sainte-Félicie-du-Bord, and although it was illegible, he feigned interest. "You can stay at my place," he said reddening. "There's a small room with a kitchen. No fireplace in the room, but the weather's not cold yet."

Slowly collapsing onto her suitcase, legs splayed, arms crossed, Judith Prunelle explained in a voice not unlike an adolescent male's, that she did not need anyone. She could find her own lodging. Then she snatched off her beret and scratched her head: "Well, whadd're ya lookin' at?"

"Um, just resting," he answered awkwardly. "I'm just back from catechism, but I'll be on my way now. Confession today. . ." Before hopping on his bike, he appeared to hesitate a moment. Then, as Judith Prunelle was still looking at him sullenly, he said in a rush, "Maybe we could swap. You find me students for catechism, and I'll put you up and give you grammar lessons."

"Don't need grammar lessons," she said. "Don't need you."

"Math maybe?"

"I know how to figure," said Judith. "Don't needja."

"Ah, well," said the priest, "if that's the way it is . . ." He left in the direction of the bushes, and Judith heard his parting voice, concerned: "Night's coming on. Got to get back."

"I ain't afraid," she said into the void. "Ain't afraid o' the night," but she was alone on the road, with dark fields in front of her and a heavy sky overhead, when she heard the murmur of wind in the leaves. She shivered and sighed, still hopeful: "Holy Mother of God, gotta find that Inspector," and she set off.

When she finally found it, the school was closed, so she opened it again. Since there was no inspector to be found, she decided to spend the night on the bare floor. "Jesus-Mary-and-Joseph, it's cold," she whimpered, her coat over her head all night long, her neck bent against the suitcase that served as a pillow. "Tomorra at dawn I've gotta light that goddam stove! Then I've gotta find some students: no students, no school. Dad was right. What the hell good's a diploma? The North's poor as the devil . . . don't need no diploma. So 'm I gonna cram some history or geometry into their little heads? I know all the dates by heart, I do. I'm no moron like he thinks, that little wise-ass priest! I know my stuff, he'll see. Charles II the Bald, Charles the Fat, Charles III, Charles the Fair. I got them all at the tips o' my fingers. Yes, Mister Priest . . . and Charlemagne too. Can you believe how cold it is in here . . . and me with no mittens! Suitcase full o' carrots, though. Useful, by Christ, but not hot! Then there's Charles IX and Charles X. I'll beat it into their ignorant little heads. Then we'll have a chorus of carrot-eating. Boy-oh-boy, all the guys in the village were bawling like calves when they saw I was leavin'. Took off their hats. Now that's respect, by God. Maybe I oughta gone back to the woods and cut trees . . . warm sun up that way. Drank beer, too, but always as skinny as a rake. More I drank, thinner I got. Charles the Bold, they gotta know that one at least . . . otherwise, it's a whack of the cane. Well, I'll be . . . if it isn't the sun. How about that for a surprise! Now that's good. I'll just shake a leg, eat a carrot and get in some wood. This is the life! Free as a bird, and I get paid, too. If only that damn Inspector General would get here.

Judith sat on the dusty desk munching a carrot, her hair still bundled under the wool beret. In fact, what she was sitting on was nothing less than the school's own history, a board where Jean-Le Maigre and the Seventh had brutishly carved their names with a knife, then signed their love-confessions in dark pencil: "Skinny Jean loves Little Hunchback Martha in life and in death"; "The Seventh requests that Miss Lorgnette wait for him after school"; "Dear Mrs. Casimir, whose bosom overfloweth with bounties, have you got a match?" (The fatal match in question was the very one that sparked a revolt and set fire to the school, but Judith Prunelle did not know this.) The new teacher aimlessly swung her legs in the hollow beneath the desk and accepted the weak ray of sun on her frozen knees: "Well now, that's what I call sunlight! Thank St. Joseph for that, at least. I was about to catch my death here. What a nasty turn that would be, bejesus! I'll have to make sure they get a few of the Charlottes, as well: Charlotte Elizabeth, Charlotte of Nassau, and all that . . . a lot of people. Better find a mat for this school of mine, too. Gotta wipe your feet before you learn history. These little snot-noses'll probably need to learn manners, and I'll have to clean the damn toilets. It's shameful the way they greet me, not even a word o' welcome from the Inspector General, either. What I think is, waitin' all this time, they've forgotten about me, but I'll give their memories a whack with the ruler. Just you wait and see."

It was six in the morning before Judith Prunelle came back from the fields with an armful of wood and kids whom she'd shaken awake in a wet barn infested with mice, a whole band of children who had taken refuge there for the night, running from a drunken grandfather who threatened to kill them and their drawn-looking mother, who no doubt was still out, as usual, begging from the silent trees: "Charity, for the love of God . . . my father's a drunk, my husband's sick, and my kids have no shoes." She also begged divine protection from a cloudless sky, which was far too peaceful to give it.

"Mama was milking the cows," Josephine Poitiers said, clutching Judith's coat with one hand. "Then, all of a sudden, she lost her mind, and to this day she's never got it back again. It runs in the family, Grampa says," continued Josephine, as she marched side-by-side with the school mistress, who was loaded down with children.

"You know, you're gonna make me fall, little girl. Then I'll tumble into the mud with all your cursed little brothers. Do you want that?"

Yet Josephine kept on anyway, pulling at Judith Prunelle's sleeve and explaining gravely: "These things happen just the same, don't they, Miss? It's God's blessing that sent you to the school. We're really going to be glad. I saw an apparition yesterday in the barn. Our Lady told me you were coming . . ."

"I don' know what you're talking about, little girl," Judith Prunelle said sharply as she put the children down. "I ain't here to save orphans. Jesus-Mary-and-Joseph, I've got a school to look after!"

"But she's going to get better, you know," said Josephine wisely.

"Grampa loves us," she said, taking her little brothers by the hand. "It's not his fault. He always feels like beating us when he's drunk." Although she had always been poor and was frequently beaten by the old man, Josephine had none of the telltale marks or deep scars that show on the faces of victims, and that separate the eternally from the temporarily unhappy. Dirty from head-to-toe (the teacher had already spotted the line of lice that outlined the little girl's pony tails, better known as "rat tails") Josephine wore dirt like an elegant gown, just as she surprised one with her delicate manners and her porcelain eyes, which she opened wide with each solemn pronouncement, seeming as it did to well up from another world and, above all, another person.

"You believe you're some lady, don't you, by Christ! I don't know if we're gonna get along," snapped the teacher with wild impatience, "and besides, I ain't got enough carrots for you all. What's his name, anyway?" she said, pointing to the smallest boy, who was wiping his nose with his fingers. "Don't look too bright."

"That's Chester," said Josephine Poitiers politely. "He's crazy, too, but Grampa says he was born that way. There are lots of idiots in the village, Miss. You have to get used to it. In our case, it runs in the family. Chester, don't wipe your nose in front of the Mistress. She doesn't like it."

"Oh, he can do it all he wants. Do I look like a princess?" Opening the school door with emphasis, she yelled, "So, this is my school. Better get started while it's still warm." Thus Josephine, Chester, Marie-Ange and Hector Poitiers sat in a circle around Judith Prunelle, listening to her talk about her favourite subject, the Creation of the World.

While she was re-creating it, waving her bony fists at the blackboard, Chester imagined his mother wandering through the fields, or tearing her bare feet on paving stones: bloody, solitary feet tracking along the white road. Josephine smiled, sometimes whispering to Chester or Hector, "Don't make so much noise with your nose. Miss doesn't like it."

Judith interrupted her lesson briefly: "Jesus-Mary-and-Joseph, a nose doesn't bother me. I don't notice it. Make all the noise you want, Chester." Josephine got up to explain, but Miss asked her to sit down, and the lesson went on. Chester closed his eyes.

"Imagine, there wasn't a monkey, not even a mushroom or a drop of rain. Betcha can't! Well, there was emptiness everywhere: not even an ant, not even a caterpillar."

"And God created the world in seven days," said Josephine Poitiers, "and on the seventh, he rested. Father Lacloche told me that, Our Lady too. Yesterday, she spoke to me. She was standing on a manure pile, and she had golden hair. She was beautiful. She said, 'Josephine, my baby is thirsty. Will you boil some milk for him?' I ran into the house, but there was no milk left, and when I came back, Our Lady was gone."

"Will you please sit down," said Judith, causing Josephine to fall off her chair. "This isn't a classroom. It's a pigpen!"

"I saw her four times in the barn," said Josephine. "She promised to come back. She said, 'Josephine, you will be most unhappy. Each night, I'd hide some bread under my pallet, if I were you. There will be famine in the village. In the meantime, pray.'"

". . . and in those days, there was no smoke nor fire," Judith battled on enflamed. "There wasn't nothin'. Then, all of a sudden, it just happened, like someone having a laugh in the middle of the night. The streams and seas and rivers, all o' that, just started bubblin' an' ragin' like fury, like soup that's boilin' over, children. It was a wonder to see . . ."

". . . and the lion lay down with the lamb," interrupted Josephine, "the wolf in the arms of the deer. Our Lady shed many tears. I have to tell you, Miss, my brothers don't wash too often. But lots of folks don't, Grampa says. Anyway, I asked Our Lady what her name was, and she said, 'Josephine, I am called Our Lady of Small Change.'"

Marie-Ange and Hector were asleep on the bench. Chester, whose square head loomed over the others, seemed to be meditating under his long lids, as shady as umbrellas. While the mistress overflowed with glistening images, and the seas overran their shores, Chester drooled on, calmly but copiously, till his shirt-collar was soaking.

"It's nothing, Miss. He dribbles. It runs in the family."

"Runs in the family," Chester seemed to echo, nodding his head.

Josephine talked so insatiably — and yet with such wisdom and moderation — that her brothers, prompted by inner laziness, never uttered a word, except once in a while to say, "Oh Josephine!" as though they were deeply astonished. Finally, they slipped into complete silence, and Chester . . . well, he just drooled more and more, which seemed to confirm Our Lady's prophecy:

"'Josephine, your brother Chester's got a very large head for his age; he's going to come to a bad end. He'll be the village idiot. I hope that doesn't upset you too much.' So I said to Our Lady, 'You're lucky, aren't you, that your baby hasn't got a big head like Chester's.'"

". . . and the fishes," persevered the mistress, "were dancing, and the birds in Spring were flying everywhere on wings as fine as paper. There were giraffes, too, marching delicately across the fresh lawn, without making a single sound."

"Was there a sky over them?" asked Josephine, rising to ask her question. "Was God there, seated on his throne of clouds? Oh yes, he was," know-it-all Josephine answered herself. "He said, 'My dear mountains, my dear hills . . .'"

"Toilet break," yelled Judith Prunelle, pushing Chester toward the door. "Aren't you ashamed, doin' that in my class, the very first day, right in the middle of the Creation of the World, and the storms and the thunder . . ."

"These things happen, Miss," said Josephine, dabbing at a suspicious-looking puddle under the bench. "I have to say, Miss, this often happens to him, but I've always got lots of hankies."

She was still babbling like a mountain stream, when Father Philippe appeared on the doorstep with a wool blanket under his arm. He cast a weary, sleepless eye on Judith Prunelle. "My child," his almost sinister voice intoned, "I've just given the last rites to poor Horace. He breathed his last in my arms."

Not knowing what to say, Judith had a moment of revulsion, then said frostily, "Well, Father, I don't know this Horace, now, do I? Besides, everyone's dyin' these days, for Chrissake! You an' me, we all gotta go, don't we? Not my fault, is it?"

"Quiet, just a moment," he begged, putting his hand to his head, "Just one moment, please."

"And is that all you've got to say about my school? No congratulations, nothin'? Boy, that's a let-down!"

"Congratulations, of course," said the priest. "It's admirable, especially at seven in the morning. I didn't come to bother you during class, but I thought you might be cold and . . ."

Judith snatched the woollen blanket from him and murmured a hurried thanks. Then, she added, "Didn't think to bring some bread, I suppose. These little beggars gotta eat. Sit down, everybody," she bawled at the kids, who had got up to greet the priest, "No special carryin' on for a priest!"

Only Josephine remained standing: "My name's Josephine Poitiers," she said with authority. "It is a blessing from God to have you in our parish, Father. We'll all be grateful. Since Father Lacloche left, the village has been sad. Everyone's been crying, though Grampa says they're happy too. This is Chester, and Marie-Ange, and Hector Poitiers. They weren't with me in the barn, when I saw Our Lady all dressed in red, holding her baby in her arms.

"Our Lady?" asked the priest, surprised.

"Oh yes," said Josephine, "Our Lady of the Blueberries. She sat down right next to me on the straw, and we ate blueberries."

"Well, we'll discuss this later," said the priest calmly. "Do you know your prayers? Have your little brothers done their catechism with Father Lacloche?"

"I taught them," said Josephine. "I also taught Father Lacloche when he came over to drink with Grampa Poilu. Grampa told me not to talk to you, because you don't drink."

"Oh, so that's it," said the priest, "I get it now."

But Josephine chirped away like a bird on a branch: "I'd really like to confess," she said. "I know everyone else's sins, too. Chester, wipe your nose. The Father doesn't like that. I met Our Lady of the Green Peas in a field the other day. Chester, your nose! She'd lost her bowl. She said to me, 'Josephine, you should found a convent right here among the peas and radishes, and gather together all the village idiots to instruct them in the ways of the Lord . . .' Then I saw a fire in the sky, and Our Lady said, 'Don't be afraid, Josephine, it's the dragon of faith descending on your house. If I were you, I'd run into the kitchen and see if Grampa's breath is on fire.' I ran in. Grampa had drunk a whole bottle of whisky, so I told him the story of St. Gondrian to put him to sleep. 'Ah, St. Gondrian,' said Grampa, 'Sure, I know him. How's he doing? By the way, Josephine, where's your mother? She's getting fat,' he said. 'What'll become of us? If I wasn't so drunk, I'd go looking for her.' I took his hand and said, 'Let's go find Mama. Our Lady will tell us where she is. She tells me everything.' Grampa was crying, and he said, 'The saints don't do us no favours these days. Used to be, your St. Gondrian'd put a bottle of whisky under my pillow every mornin'.' Then I said, 'Walk straight, Grampa. What's Mama going to say if she sees you like this?'

"'I got a gun', said Grampa, 'Pow! Pow! Pow! I could blow all your brains out. Ah, just be quiet and let me drink in peace. Too many kids in this world. I could sleep forever, snorin' away happily.' Grampa was crying. He was all broken up after killing his little Josephine. 'Hey, there's yer mother,' he said, wiping away his tears so he could see her better. 'Rose, come here. Let me take you in my arms, my refuge, my heart. What's happened to you? You look so strange. How'd you cut your feet like that?'

"'Dear, Sweet Josephine,' Mama said, sitting in the middle of the road, 'Have you looked after the cow? Did you boil milk for the baby?' I have to tell you, Father, when we got home, we wiped the blood off her feet and put her to bed.

"But then, all of a sudden, Grampa got in a fearful rage and pulled his gun down off the wall and said, 'Chester? Where is that kid? I'll kill him!'" "Chester, Chester," whined Josephine, suddenly weeping through her own story, and upsetting both the Father and Judith Prunelle, who were watching her, "Chester . . . Grampa put holes in him everywhere!"

Seeing he was dead, Chester started crying too. Then all the Poitiers children joined in noisily, until Judith whacked her yardstick twice against the blackboard and reduced them to silence. "Jesus-Mary-and-Joseph," she cried, "Where'm I at? Would you mind tellin' me? What on earth are we goin' to do with this school, Father?"

Father Philippe just shrugged his shoulders.

Act of
Pity

FOR A LONG TIME, the curate of Vallée d'Or had felt himself giving way to a complacency born of long-standing ambition and piously nurtured pride. After all, he gave a little shudder of secret joy, didn't he, when spreading his stiff compassion among those around him, when feeling the humble gratitude of the poor transformed into murmurs of praise: "Ah, the Father's the finest man on the surface of the Earth," or, "Never in a hundred years could we find another priest like him . . ."

Yet, on this particular morning, as he strode toward the Sansfaçon cabin, he knew death would be waiting; he knew he was not simply going to entertain Maria or tell stories to raise her from her fevered bed with laughter, but to convey a last blessing as he closed her eyes. A weariness invaded him at this thought, as though he realized that the mere appearance of saintliness — his shining reputation in the village — was nothing, since he did not deserve it; in five years of ministry, his heart had never really known pity. He had, of course, loved God with a fervour that pleased his cool, priestly vanity, but he had never been able to approach real people simply and without disgust. He thought of Maria's pallid life, about to expire in her soiled bed, like so many other young lives in the village, taken away by consumption . . . and the same disgust made its shuddering return. "But it's too late," he thought, "I've fallen far too much in love with their false impression of me . . ." How many times had he faked charity, compassion, or even love, and repressed deep within himself the terrible nausea inspired by other people's infirmity — his heart hardened with princely disdain, while all the while doing good so as to store up the words, "Our priest's Christ Himself on Earth," and get positively drunk on them later. This ideal of sweet superiority had, of course, demanded certain sacrifices. He could not live in the lap of luxury like some of his confreres in neighbouring parishes. He had no more than a roof over his head, and yet he could not help feeling that his spare existence had called up an exaggerated sense of his own importance, a sort of pleasure in his own austerity and abstinence, which he ought to disapprove of, but after which he hungered. Seated without bread at the tables of his flock, he had fasted with them, all the while thinking of the light repast that would greet his return at evening; if he had partaken of the silence of hunger, it had been while thinking of himself and his sanctified image with others . . . still without being moved by the miserable hovels he visited.

Scrawny fields, a village crushed under drought and a burning sky, children begging like dogs the moment he appeared — was this the frail empire he had dreamed for himself? Still, there was only one crying need that truly offended him, one that he could not answer: pity — that he always denied. "Is it my fault, this wall of ice between them and me . . . this distance of privilege? No, more than just that," he thought. It was more than the distance imposed by anxiety and disgust: he thoroughly despised them. These subjugated women, these ageless men resigned to the premature deaths of their sons, like the ravages of seasons — none of them inspired the slightest compassion in him.

"Ah, Father, we ain't been lucky this year . . ." but he knew he was reigning over a roost of eternal victims.

"Of course, the prematurely dead have no fight in them," he thought, walking like one who was crushed himself, "and they've been pitiless with me, too, overpowering me with their trust, and especially their ignorance. They've imposed their misery on me without ever wanting to be cured."

"Mornin', Father. Goin' to see the Sanschagrin kid, are ye? They're dyin' real quick over that way . . . contagious, y'know."

"Seems the Létourneaus' baby's dyin', too."

Tournemule bursts out laughing. "Ah, Father, quicker yer born, quicker ye die. C'mon over, me old mother'd like yer blessin' 'fore she crosses over."

"I'll come tomorrow," replies the priest, controlling his anger at the idea that God could create such a beautiful landscape, such a promise of serenity and joy (he could see the sea far off, across the burnt fields with their fruitless trees) to have it yield only destitution and decay.

"Go home, Tournemule, your mother's all alone. Tell her I'll come tomorrow," but Tournemule only hangs on to the cassock with grey hands. "Well, what do you want?" asks the priest. Tournemule has no idea: a miserable caress? a look? The priest bends his head slightly toward the blind man's forehead, taking care not to touch it, nor to meet the ravaged eyes under their wide, staring lids: "You're no longer a child, Tournemule. Go on home."

He had spoken firmly, but in a voice vibrant with a seeming charity that reassured the lowly Tournemule, caged in shadow and night, where he still heard his mother's sickly cries: "Tournemule! Tournemule! Where is he? Gone and left me alone. Tournemule! Tournemule!"

"You see, Father, she calls me day and night. No peace at all. Poor mother, she never stops howlin' my name."

"Have pity on her," said the Father, coolly sensing his own disdain. He slipped away, while Tournemule murmured something odd, which he muffled with his fingers.

Before knocking at the Sansfaçons' door, he stopped for a second, just at the threshold. The intimacy of the suffering and grief disgorged by the houses in Vallée d'Or now had him trembling with anxiety. Far off, in the deep blue sky, a cloud hung immobile; the air was so hot, one could barely breathe. Thick clusters of flies buzzed over a pile of offal in the garden. "Not a flower, not a bird, everywhere drought and death . . ."

"Father, what're you doin' out here in this heat?" cried a woman's voice. "You've got to give her extreme unction, Father. She's lost a lot of blood . . ."

There was no escape now, as the woman dragged him into the house. Never raising his eyes, he walked to Maria's bedside, pushing aside whatever scraggly children lay in his way, sensing the smell of the disenfranchised, the abandoned. "Hasn't the doctor been?" he asked.

"Don't need no doctor," said the mother. "Kid's gonna die."

"Die like flies, they do," said her husband, rocking a little one on his knee. "Don't know what gets into them in summer. It's like they choke . . ."

"The sun, that's what it is," the mother said sadly, going to her daughter's bedside, sitting down, then stroking her hair while she chased away flies. "Maria, your friend, the Father, has come. Now, don't make that face. Open your eyes."

Soon the mother's voice became impatient and tired: "She used to be such an angel, Father. Now, all of a sudden, she's mean, stubborn enough to try the patience of a saint. Maria, can you hear what I'm sayin'?"

"You hear your mother?" joined in the husband with a hint of tender sadness that surprised the priest, "Well, d'ye hear your mother, Maria?"

The priest waved a hand for silence around the girl, approaching her and wanting to touch her hand, but pulling back immediately. "She doesn't like me any more," he thought. "She knows all about my struggle. She knows, as God knows, how hard my heart is." Terrified by Maria's silence and by the fierce look she suddenly shot at him, he spilled out words so clumsy that he regretted them at once: "Are you suffering much, Maria?"

She bit her lip and said nothing. For a moment at least, she seemed to forget about him, as she watched the beams of light flutter ineffectually across the bed.

"You remember when we were friends, don't you?" he said, but she did not. If he was her friend, how could he let her die like this? How could he bless all these tortures she felt?

"Maybe it's the fear of hell," said her mother.

"God preserve you," said the priest, short on words of consolation, for he knew there was nothing left to do but entrust Maria to Him. It was too late . . . or maybe too soon; the time for pity had not yet come. "How many souls of children are there in this limbo of disgust? They haunt me, all of them, and yet I've never loved them . . ." He looked at Maria, still lost in the air of dreamy obstinacy which she had turned on him, and forgot that she had already ceased to live moments before, lost in oblivion, in that bitter indifference where the stifled appeal of a body, gasping from the blows of an invisible executioner, could no longer reach him.

"Maria, Maria," said her mother in a low voice . . .

"Don't you hear your mother?" said her father from the other end of the room. At the sound of his voice, loud and begging, the child on his knee began to cry. The father slapped it, and it was silent, but another yellow-haired child began crying, too. The father looked weary and said nothing.

"Dead," her mother said.

The rest of the children gathered round the bed. They were not frightened by the all-too-familiar spectacle. All of them watched the thread of blood from Maria's silent mouth. "Degenerate creatures from the dawn of time," the priest thought sadly, "carriers of vermin, sickness and corruption . . ." but these pressed close to him and begged with their starving eyes.

"Oh Father, please don't go!"

Suddenly, one of his nightmares came back to him. It was Sunday morning, time for communion, and the faithful all knelt before him, awaiting the Host; their mouths were wide open, indecently he thought, and as he leaned towards those miserable, gaping faces, he could see all the infected sores in their throats. Barely had he placed the wafer on the tongue of an old woman from Vallée d'Or when she at once showed her teeth like a ferocious beast. "They're eating me, devouring me," he thought. When he awoke, he was frozen with anxiety and fear. He knew all the symptoms of his weakness immediately. They should be feeding on him, not on God, and he did not give of himself. Yet, while he slept, he was theirs. One day, he would have to relent and lose himself in the abjectness of his flock. ("My flock! Why?" he thought, "they're even more unknown to me than I am myself.") He would disappear totally in it to the point of no longer being. ("But that kind of compassion would be suicide, and I want to live . . .")

As he left Maria's house, he could still hear her mother quietly sobbing behind him. Oh, to regain the cool of the church, to lose himself in solitude . . . It was too hot to pray, even to be alive. He was still thirsty, with a sudden, violent thirst, but water was scarce in this calcinated countryside. At times like this, he thought that he lived in a drought that was even greater than his resistance to suffering. Was he not completely abandoned, even by God? He, like his church, was empty and alone, so aloof that nothing could trouble him. Christ dying on His cross was nothing more than an image of suffering doled out unfairly. He stared at the cross as he had Maria's face a few hours earlier, thinking, "When will all this agony be over?"

He had hoped that the intent stride of his youth, impelled by his forsworn love of happiness, would carry him away forever from all the misery he had seen without ever being able to help. Failed saintliness had also meant failed happiness. He no longer loved the man he had once been, clothed in seeming goodness, fed on illusions which finally had fooled no one so much as himself. "If only the children of Vallée d'Or had been true children of God, not merely the offspring of his shame and humiliation . . ."

Closing his eyes, he had a vision of Maria running towards him. "Why are your knees bloody again, Maria?"

"Mama says it's because I'm so weak I fall whenever I try to run . . . Father, Father, don't walk so fast!" She called out to him, but he refused to hear.

"These are the stigmata of children in Vallée d'Or," he thought, "Not once could I see them without thoughts of running away . . . but is it really my fault one can't caress a child in this village without feeling nauseous?" Its misery, its stench and its hunger would cling to one, permeate one. "Lord, You who made them so humble and helpless, how am I supposed to love them?" Could he, in a surge of vanity, still find the strength to lie . . . just to hear those words: "Our Father's a real saint"? He could play the martyr, but since Maria's death, a strange weariness had overtaken him . . .

How often he had pushed her away when he had found her waiting for him on the church steps at evening: "Maria, I want to be alone, and here you are, chattering like a magpie."

"But I've got some things to tell you."

"You can tell me in the morning," but he knew that she would no longer be there. He had already noticed, during catechism, Maria's pallid face, as she coughed up blood. How many kids in Vallée d'Or coughed and spat the same way! The tortured note of those coughs tormented his nights, tearing the curtain of silence around his dreams.

"You mustn't spit on the floor, Maria. Here, take my handkerchief." He might have added, "This is the sum of all I will ever give you in your short life."

People died on their feet in Vallée d'Or, and it was only at the beginning of the end that Maria could curl up in her mother's bed.

"Maria talked to me in the evening, but what did she say? I wasn't listening; the sound of her voice grated, and I couldn't look at her without feeling guilty."

"Father. Father." That evening, other children called out to him, but Maria was no longer one of them. Forgetfully, absent-mindedly, he had simply let her die . . .

The priest was suffocating between the walls of his room. The day had been too long. The sun was slowly going down over barren fields. Standing motionless by the window, he neglected to eat the meagre supper of vegetables and bread waiting for him on the table. For several days now, such a deep disgust had settled on him that the bread sitting there seemed all of a sudden like the rotting flesh of Vallée d'Or. All around him, the limitless, bare, desiccated landscape seemed to reflect his own desolation. "Lord, may I possess nothing but the ardour of my own soul, and spare me all satisfaction," — this had been the prayer of his mortified youth. He looked at the brass bed against the white wall, the crucifix, the wretched table, and he understood that he had not lived simply, but greedily: "Of course, I only did it for fear of having to look at the things I owned, or more likely, I was afraid of being owned by them." He had despised poverty, while loving its privileges and its honours:

"Pious words roll so easily off dying lips."

"Fahder, our saviour."

"Fahder . . . it's me Tournemule!"

"What is it now?" the priest inquired as he opened his door to the blind man, who was fairly bobbing with laughter.

"It's me poor mother who's askin' for ye, Father, she's afraid of getting through the night . . ."

"At nightfall, she always worries about dying. Tell her I'll be there tomorrow."

"But she's really scared, Fahder, and she's swearin' like the devil. Lookit how I'm shakin'!"

"You're the one who's afraid, Tournemule. Why must you always lie?" Then, looking at the half-eaten bread on his table, he said, "Here, take this bread, Tournemule. I'm not feeling hungry tonight." A few minutes later, he was ahead of Tournemule on the dusty road. The heat still hung on, but night would soon fall.

"My child, my child," he said to the old woman, delirious on her shadowy bed. "It is late, it is time to think of repentance," but Tournemule's mother instead howled with anger: "I'm thirsty. I don't want to die!" and she suddenly broke into a strange good humour, a savage joy with a hint of evil.

"Sshhh . . . you're not making any sense," he said.

Yet she went on with her rambling monologue: "Tournemule tried to kill me — yes he did — with a pick one day, an' another day with an axe. Tell the truth, Tournemule. Oh, I don't like that one bit! I'd have scratched his eyes out like a little cat.

"She's thirsty," said the priest. "Give her something to drink." With a trembling hand, Tournemule gave it to her, then, dipping his hand in the water bucket, he stroked the old woman's cheeks and forehead: "Don't be afraid, poor old Mother. I'm just goin' to cool you off."

As though recalling an old habit, she touched his eyes like a small child. "I'm tellin' you, Father, this bad boy wanted to kill me. That's right . . . cut my throat! Go on, tell the Father the truth, Tournemule!"

"It's no longer time to be thinking of hate," said the priest, "You have been through such unhappiness and want together. Who knows, perhaps there's still a spark of that old tenderness somewhere under all the ashes. You must think of that and of nothing else." ("Hypocrite," he thought, "saying words you don't feel, and probably never have, except maybe today, when finally you were faced with Maria's cruel dignity.")

The old woman died at daybreak, still accusing her son with joyous indecency, then finally letting herself be wafted away, sad and broken, in the calm eye of her madness. Later that night, he dreamed of purging his sins by setting fire to the church, but God wanted still more. He was to gather all the children of Vallée d'Or, down to the smallest, remove his priest's attire, quit himself at last of the religious appearances in which he lived, and naked as any

beggar, wander the roads, sick, weary and pleading not for bread
— which could not nourish his soul — but for renewal, the truth of
a single act of pity.

"Tournemule, where are you going? I need you, any of you who
can teach me poverty." But Tournemule was busy pushing a black-
ened cart ahead of him. His face was not visible, but the two narrow shoulders were wracked with nervous shuddering: "Look at
me, Tournemule."

"Too late, Father. Night's comin' on. Got to bury me poor old
mother." Like a drunken man, he sang:

> Long live a mother brave,
> gone one morning to her grave.
> Long live a mother brave,
> Tournemule, Tournemule,
> of an axe, a dream I have . . .

The words of the song were swallowed up by the hot air, and
soon Tournemule's shadow disappeared completely from the
scrubby hillside. The priest knelt down to pray, but no acknowl-
edgement of God would spring to his lips. He saw Maria walking
towards him, as in days before, but this time it was she who offered
him bread. He wanted to talk to her, keep her with him for a few
moments, for never had he known such abandonment, such solitude, but already she was gone. He took a bite of the poor and
tasteless bread, and as he ate, icy blood streamed between his fingers.

When he awoke, he was crying and repeating over and over that
tears, once cowed by his indifference, were at last flowing from
him. It did him good to feel this shame lifted. For an instant, he
believed his void of pity would soon be filled, enabling him to do
great things in Vallée d'Or: "Oh, how proud they'll be of their
priest, these people . . ." The pride of this thought at once saddened him. In the midst of repentant tears, was he still in love with
this image of himself . . . this void? Was this really all that mattered?

"Eat, eat this bread," had said the voice in his dreams. What if this food, instead of life, brought him death? Admitting his weakness was a miraculous awakening, to be sure, but it could not stop him from lying or concealing his hardness of heart from the rest of the world. "Tomorrow, once again, I'll say to Tournemule, 'Tell me the truth,' and demand of him virtues that I lack myself. I'll offer Maria's mother consolation, but not love. I . . ."

But did God Himself have pity? What could we possibly know of that distant, invisible pity so rarely expressed? "Of course God's pity is symbolic, but if it were alive before me forever, like a fervent example, how could I commit the sin of injustice a hundred times each day?"

Sitting on the edge of his bed, he looked at his hands, so clean and white. "Never will my hands be worn and grey like Tournemule's. Never will I cough up blood like Maria. God's protecting me too well! Little by little, he became indifferent to his own tears. It was hot in the room. Flies stuck to the window. Day was dawning, just as suffocating as yesterday. If, all of a sudden, the priest sensed a timid sort of pity, it may have been too late. There was no one to receive it.

Dispossession

HE KNEW HE WAS NO longer a person, just a cursed, despicable thing of battered flesh, sitting there on a pile of newspapers and surrounded by a crowd that wanted nothing to do with him, barely even noticed him amid the blind turbulence of the storm that swept the city. A trace of drunkenness still nerved his limbs, which were stiffened by cold, and in a last grasp at life — as though sensing that the world of the living he was about to quit was already dissolving into distant memory — he stretched out his arms to them in a futile plea, waging to the end his silent war on the world, a passive, lonely war against the imminent degradation, disintegration and extinction of that pathetic creature he had become in so little time . . . in a world he was never really part of, in a country where he was a born exile. These men, these women and children, grey or flashing stains in the blinding fog, dived into cars or hurried to the comfort of home in sky-scrapers between city and pale sky, and he felt their shoes and boots stumbling into him, but feverish, he no longer said, "Leave me alone . . . you have no idea how much I hate you all!" as he had so many times before, when he was still able to walk along with leftovers begged from restaurants wrapped

49

in rags and newspapers under his arm. Now, he was too weak for hate. The February wind sliced through the tattered sleeves of his jacket; yet still he held out his arms to passers-by, as his face was covered with freezing saliva, and bits of newspaper were whipped around him by the blast of snow. They came and went, cowed by the storm, apparently without seeing him. Surely he was not yet invisible, this shameful stain on a great, industrial, North American city. Maybe he ought to beg harder, moan perhaps, but his voice was barely more than a scraping sound in his chest. Gradually the cold wrapped his limbs in numbness, and he worried about falling asleep. He thought of the shelters he had known in his wanderings, havens with filthy beds, and more recently, hotel doorways and park benches — magnets for drunks and junkies with haggard faces, young people already looking ravaged, faces that weighed on him, as though present all around him in the glacial vapour rising from the earth, the exhalations of young life mixing with his own last breath. Then suddenly, it seemed he would like to live after all, but there was no possible place for him to go . . . no place but shelters and more shelters, constantly on the alert, as though waiting for the inevitable bombs to fall. In the shadows of a world belonging only to others, he often had a vague sense he was still fighting, but for what? He could not explain this warlike tension that had been his life in such a peaceful and prosperous country. Perhaps he was nothing more than a drunk, a degenerate, an illiterate, but he also felt he was the victim of a hidden and unnameable war. Otherwise, how could they not have noticed his desolation and misery? The storm was worsening, and all he could make out were shapes bending into the wind, each one rushing far away. "I mustn't go to sleep," he thought. "Soon they won't see me at all," and the sombre blanket of snow, gradually enveloping his body as night fell, also covered his eyes, little by little. A heavy sleep began to creep upon him, but his eyes were still open, and he wept softly. Then he heard the distant siren of an ambulance, and hope returned: a couple of policemen would come to rescue him, take him to hospital, where kind hands would help him to bits of bread soaked in warm milk. Safe . . . he would be saved. They could not just let him die here in dreadful loneliness, could they, this revolting bundle dumped on the sidewalk, this human debris undeserving of attention or sympathy when, all around him, a multitude of people marched toward their innocence, their happiness and pleasure? Then he could hear nothing. Suddenly, the city seemed deserted: the police, the social worker who had so often found him shelter, that unknown, ordinary man whose simple, quiet pity — there were still good people like that — yes, the man who, a few days ago, had held him close to warm him and said, "I'll call a doctor. What's happened to you? I thought things like this only happened in the Third World . . . not here, especially not here," . . . all of them stood around him, saying, "Don't worry. You'll be O.K." Anticipating the tender gestures that seemed slow in coming, he stretched his arms out in front of him, bending forward slightly: "Almost asleep," he thought, his eyes closing already — they would come. "Yes," he thought, "I hear them coming," but the faces were merely faint apparitions in the white of night. No one came.

Tenderness

THE TWO WOMEN SLEPT gently entwined. They had met just hours before and shared only a few words and brief caresses; yet now the room was filled with their presence, the sensual intimacy of their bodies, their lives warming together against the cold March night. While outside the icy spring downpour could be heard, inside the smell of rain and fog still clung to their clothes — coats too heavy, shoes weighted down with mud, at one moment dire necessities, the next shed and scattered as they crossed the threshold, borne in on a whirlwind of sensuality. Now they were asleep, or pretending to be, glances and hands still seeking one another in the warm sanctuary of the bed. Suddenly a pang of tenderness, but nervousness at feeling love for someone new, a first embrace in the night — all of it had taken them by surprise, rooted them together in an oasis neither had ever been to before. Perhaps there was nowhere else that sisterhood, a virgin union, could take place, and when dawn's dull light effaced the luminous gestures of night, would not each go her way, as always, and do just what she had to?

Soon enough, summer morning would dazzle them . . . why not wait before saying goodbye? Their closed eyes gradually awoke with tentative, fervent glances, drawn together in summer's glow, cheeks hot, eyes shining with fugitive hope, life, summer, us, time of abandonment and love immobilized in this room . . . all the time, knowing chill isolation waited for them outside. One of them asked herself what she liked so much in the other . . . was it the obstinate lock of hair that fell over her longish ear or her small, firm foot, muscled and ready for the race — race or flight? — which she had delightedly held between her fingers? Still, in the pastures of abandon that night had laid before them, she felt she already knew the other's body: salt tears at eyelid corners, a familiar taste, for at the edges of the other's eyes, her own soul perched, suddenly attentive, vigilant, and holding her own drunkenness in suspense (and she thought, "She's just penetrated me, suddenly, impetuously. Of course I'll love her. How else could it be?") from the tears held back to the vigour of this narrow foot that made her smile, yes, every detail of this body joyously explored, didn't it hold you aching to her, because you have to know everything, understand at least this reigning chaos that bursts into our lives.

Perhaps her companion was cold or in a hurry to leave: "Cover your shoulders", as though they had always spoken to each other this way, murmuring in a low voice, but with veiled authority, an order to one already dimly thought of as "my friend". Yet the kindliness of such words and gestures could have been shown to other lovers on many nights like this. She put her lips to the crease that lined the other's cheek, drank the bitter tears, sensed the solitary, skittish fragments of past lives passing between them in the voluptuous air that filled the room. A sudden chill caused the other to pull the sport shirt over her breasts, hiding a torso of child-like beauty (when her companion had just talked about how all living things deteriorated with suffering and time, and her words still inhabited the room with their sober modesty and served to shelter crumbling days of splendour) this thing, this piece of blue cotton that draped the other's body against shivering cold, became in the first glow of dawn, her flesh and scent, every imprint of her. The shirt, with its short, frayed sleeves — as though clawed by her lover's impatient hands (and the yellowed patches worn to transparency under the arms, where a down was visible, darkening as though, under the coals of her body, still other fires burned, quietly smouldering . . . clothes merely serving to subject them to the dictates of cold weather) this pale blue garment, now framed in the light of dawn, breathed with her, listening like a lover's ear to the beating of her heart. Now, all of a sudden, instead of shielding her from the cold, it slipped away, unveiling, charm after charm, the musculature of her stomach, strong enough to support her lover's head, her hard thighs and her foot, so irrepressible and strong in its longing to start up, to be in motion, that the loving fingers could no longer still it, but had to let it soar to its own dreams or careworn nervousness. Is not the body like the rest of us . . . complicated, stubborn in its resistance against the pathetic restraints that keep us from soaring to freedom?

The day dawned with a violence of grey light and chill wind that had blown down trees in the night, and it separated hands still warm and hesitant to join once again, for they had to leave, but there was still the hope in their eyes, as when they had slept in each other's arms — though not really slept — spying out what they longed for through half-closed eyelids, that all-inclusive, unspoken hope, the abundance of impulsive giving that had made them drunk, that hope — almost nothing, or perhaps everything — love, still and tomorrow, perhaps, for now, the memory of their breathing in the night.

Revolutionary
and Friend

—◇—

We have lived together
for twenty-five years,
and now it's time I told you . . .

I STILL SEE HER GETTING ready to leave. She has on a backpack and serious-looking clothes: narrow skirt and blouse with sleeves rolled up . . . under a dark green army greatcoat. That was the year race riots exploded all over the U.S., and she was going to join her black friends and fight for their rights in the southern states, where they couldn't be seen in public with whites. I still see her on T.V. in those days of bloody and tragic revolution, stepping forward, sure and determined, hand-in-hand with her friends. Of course, she's with other pacifists and students, but I know her. She's fragile and alone in the middle of the crowd . . . a hostile crowd like the ones we so often saw in the papers of the time. She is surrounded by evil presences: the Knights of the Klu Klux Klan and packs of heavily armed cops. In that prison cell in Georgia, where she and her friends run a hunger-strike for forty days, until they are force-fed, she writes every day in that fine and obstinate hand of hers, tirelessly denouncing prison conditions. She sends us these book-fragments on blue toilet paper, testimony even now, to the painstaking attention she pays to everything she does for others, a patient, rigorous humanism, which I rarely understood. I could never figure out why she had to risk her life, when she could have spent it, serene and content, in the country, with all those books and friends. What mysterious determination was it that took her away from us, from the artist-writer's contemplation that she had chosen in her youth, suddenly to live a life of struggle that seemed to be made up only of hardship and trial? When she gets out of prison, we meet her at the airport, and for the first time, I am aware of the sharp, red line that has separated black from white. People look away from a face they've seen in the papers and on T.V.; they've seen it side-by-side with Blacks, in riots, where they were all hounded and injured, where confirmed pacifists were subjected to violence and racism. That look of hatred, or of nothing at all, that flash of contempt follows us everywhere . . . to the motel, where she tries to rest . . . to the beach, under a brutal sun pitilessly burning those arms and legs, fleshless, almost transparent under the heavy coat she wears, despite the heat. After this, she will always be cold from the privation and suffering in her Georgia prison, always be cold 'til the day she dies. The last time I see her, she is still wearing a sweater and heavy boots . . . on a burning hot day in Florida.

While she doesn't eat much, to the desperation of the friends who are trying to keep her alive, she spends the whole day reading and writing by the sea, under a pale, warm sky. Her stomach still hurts from the days of fasting, and she speaks with marvellous buoyancy of the orange drink they gave her when the hunger-strike was over. A kind of sweet euphoria lingers when she talks about her friends from those days, and even that filthy prison. I listen to her with secret shame and despondency; they were beaten, clubbed, force-fed, and still she says humanity is making progress. She's barely cured when already she is taking up the argument again, underscoring it with deliberate movements of head and nervous hands, striding with determination toward the beach. Already, she has other projects in hand. Got to be off. Yesterday, with stubborn candour and implacable logic, she was discussing disarmament with Castro; tomorrow, she says she'll go with her friends and invade that fortress of terror, the Pentagon.

I still see her unfolding her sand-coloured backpack and slipping into it the narrow skirt, the blouse with rolled-up sleeves — "No-care clothes," she explains, "just wash them and put them back on" — plus a blanket and a tin cup. She has cut her hair herself, tidy and straight, with a fringe across the front; her young face already has wrinkles . . . they've come quickly to this fine and delicate skin. The limpidity and frankness in those brown eyes moves me, as does her restless, tortured intelligence when she's witnessing someone else's pain. So here she is as I see her, and after all these years, I still don't know if I understood her then . . . or do now.

On yet another trip to Washington, she camps out in a park on a rainy night and is raped by a friend. She lends her coat to another, who is later killed. Again, she is sent to prison. Through every American university rumbles the Vietnam War, preparing to harvest from those tree-flowered campuses all the young boys stretched out on the grass with their books. Just before those terrible days, we could still hear the whirring of bicycles in the streets and the choir in the university chapel at evening. In the late-lit library, they steeped themselves in philosophy, science and history; then, suddenly, the campus walks were deserted. No longer able to read on the lawn, reclining with arm under head, or looking up at the clouds, they had turned eighteen, and the thing they feared the most was upon them.

She watches these young soldiers, some of them still children, go off to kill their brothers in Asia. Enough of this waiting, agitated, in front of a work-table . . . she abandons the quiet of her house for the streets and, like all the others, rails against the war. Now she is surrounded by writers, famous poets and Catholic priests, for a new solidarity has grown out of those once tight and lonely ranks. Still, she reproaches herself for being alive while her country's decimating an entire people, napalming its villages and laying waste its fields for twenty years to come. It is then she decides to go to Vietnam, along with a group of pacifists and an Anglican priest. Her friends try to stop her: it's absurd! Why risk dying under those bombs . . . during a non-violent demonstration in a country at war? We've got to be done with this war, she says, believing in the good will of the American people to do just that. It's true . . . the image of a few pacifists being attacked by South Vietnamese police does touch the popular conscience. The protests multiply; soldiers, revolted by the massacres, desert. Yet, before the end of a war which has stained the heart with shame, what I see most of all is my friend, wrought with compassion. I see her, back from Vietnam, alone and desolate, wondering about the place of non-violence in the world, her photos splashed across the papers, along with accu-sations of treason and violent diatribes by the right-wing press against her and anyone who dares defend her. Still, this collective rage doesn't seem to affect her, convinced as she is that the war is ending. She visits her friends, imprisoned as conscientious objec-tors, writes to them and takes them into her home, while all across the country, war-resisters are being chased down. I was fortunate to know her in those seven crucial years of American history, though I often saw my friend cry, saw her despair at the Kennedy deaths, for even if she disapproved of their politics, these two horrible murders following one another in a single curse, affected her pro-foundly. For a long time, we kept a photo we'd cut out of the paper; in it, we lived and re-lived the last moments of a young Robert Kennedy, lying with his eyes wide open, in the hall where he'd just spoken so triumphantly. Vulnerable and stricken, lucid yet power-less, he looks at us, judging, like those young blonde soldiers strewn over the battlefields of Vietnam, wondering why he had to die, seeming to ask, "Who has just killed me?" or, "Am I really dying?" Her pain becomes even more apparent with the deaths, in quick succession, of Martin Luther King and Malcolm X, close allies of hers. No longer does she hide her tears. It is only a short while later that a young black friend named Ray dies (I found out later she had taken care of his wife and kids), killed in a riot on one of the campuses where white and black students have been fighting side-by-side. King, Malcolm and Ray — they are all gone now, and she begins to sink, to surround herself with work and austere reading-matter: philosophers and historians only, whom she often tries to decipher in the originals, mediocre though she's always been in languages. The shootings at Kent State seem forever to shatter her faith in non-violence as a means of humanitarian and political pressure. Yet she never turns violent, refusing to join black groups that use force; instead, she withdraws and writes. At first, she publishes books on things she's always been concerned about: prison conditions, the role of non-violent action in a violent society; then she throws herself into the radical feminist movement, and for the rest of her life, works exclusively for the cause of women. She opens a shelter for battered women and rape victims and, expressing disdain for the bourgeois class she's sprung from, she little by little gives away all she has, though she never expects others to share her abnegation. She is forever prepared to help out an artist friend, or a writer . . . anybody whose ideas might not agree with hers. Again she and her friends are arrested and jailed for trying to get through the barbed wire of a nuclear plant. One winter evening, on the way back from a pacifist meeting, she's asleep in the back seat, when they are hit by another car. Her friends are barely injured, but she is found unconscious on the floor; for a long time we're afraid for her life. She has to spend nearly a year in hospital, learning to live — barely survive — all over again in a new body made from broken bones. Her intelligence is not affected, and despite a long period of enforced lethargy, she is clear-eyed and impatient to leave the hospital. There's still a mark on her throat, where they placed a breathing-tube, and after she gets out, she'll always walk with a cane. Cold weather is so hard for her to bear that, no sooner is she home in New England, than she has to leave for the south and the sun, that same South that so abused and humiliated her. "But so much has changed since then," she says, taking pride in an evolution so small it is barely noticeable. Once again, the backpack is hoisted, but this time it appears to be for good. We help her dress, and she says goodbye with a confident smile, vulnerable, her head tilted to one side, her hair stiff and straight, for she still cuts it herself, though she's as clumsy as she ever was. Down there, on her desert island in Florida, she writes that her bones ache less, and she swims daily. She's living in a small commune of women, with dogs and cats. Every day she writes and reads a great deal. Her favourite thinkers are no longer men, but women. She says nothing of her physical suffering. For a few years we still connect through her writing, which displays the same stubbornness and logic as her speeches, along with the same unreasoning hope in the future . . . a better one in a better world. It's as though I'm still hearing her voice in front of me, and I'm arguing with her (she's far too saintly, her ideas are far too elevated, it seems to me), still with the full fire of my youth.

It is much later when we meet again, there, on her island in the south. Leaning on her cane, she appears weaker than before, though she works just as rigorously as she used to. I entertain odd doubts about the group of friends around her; she is so used to living in an ordered, studious environment, whereas these young women who have gravitated to her are untidy, often slovenly and rude (and she's so fond of gentleness and courtesy), and seem to be taking advantage of her weakened state, of her generosity and openness. My biggest criticism of them is that they don't encourage her to see a doctor, preferring instead to brew up harmful herbal drinks and keeping her from noticing the decline in her health. She reacts badly to my remarks and says the herbal teas reduce her stomach pains. "There's nothing wrong with me," she says, "I don't know why I'm complaining," but I can tell she's in great pain, that her life has been torture ever since the accident, though she denies it. I point out that the doctor, her own brother, who treated her in New York, is worried and wants her to come back for more extensive tests, but she's not listening. She just goes on drinking herbal teas, while her friends invade her space. She writes in a corner of her room, on her bed, as though she were still in prison, and eats very little. There she is, stretched languidly out on her bed, for that innate elegance goes with her everywhere. Despite herself, like her mother and her lanky brothers, she'll always be graceful beneath that unkempt and slightly masculine look, especially in those Florida winter months when she suffers from chills, always draped in a sweater or that somewhat forbidding overcoat, and wearing heavy boots, as we go down to the canal to see her boat. "This is where I come every morning," she tells me. "I go out on the water and listen to the strident birdsong." She explains every detail of her trips out on the water, her love of the solitude in this sort of jungle, where yesterday her cat was bitten by a viper. Alone in the boat, she makes notes and writes, always surprised at how quickly she gets tired. Then, one day, she can't do it any more. The cold has crept into her bones, she says, and she writhes in pain on her bed, in the middle of the cell where books and papers cascade to the floor. This time, a doctor really must be called in. She knows now, and probably has known for a long time, that the cancer is very advanced and she must go to hospital. Maybe cobalt treatment will allow her to live a year or two longer . . . but she's out of bed and gets her friends to take her home to her place by the canal. She says the treatment is useless and she'd rather die peacefully, naturally, aware of her death. When she's told there are only a few days left, she smiles confidently and seems untroubled by it: "When my suffering gets too great, just please do what you can to end it." Those days turn out to be one week, a week of stabbing pain, in which she gets up to greet friends come from the world over: family, writers, artists — a week in which she doesn't die as other people do. She eats nothing, drinks little water, and her life seems to hang by a thread, albeit a steel one. She is there for them all as she has never been before. Except for a few hours in the evening, when the reddened sun falls into the ocean and the white herons land on the canal next to her boat, she is always standing, and instead of saying, "I am going to die," she says, "Can I do something for you? I am leaving soon." And they confide in her, expecting that special — maybe superhuman — help right to the end. There are even celebrations in the two days leading up to her death, in which she amuses her friends by dressing up in various outfits she's collected in her travels: a silk tunic from China, a Peruvian hat perched on her bald head. When she's feeling stronger, sometimes in the evening, she does a dance-step she learned in Greece, where she led a youthful, happy and bohemian existence. That was when she was writing poetry and thinking little about world politics. I am not there when she gently drifts away, but I can picture them finding her body, curled up to ward off the pain, under the white cotton sheet — for it's been a very warm night, and perhaps she didn't feel cold. They've given her the pain-killer she asked for, so she could get to sleep: "Oh, it's O.K. You can give me more. I'm so very tired tonight." The exaltation of the healing fluid was in her veins, and it masked the pain in her bones, but just barely, because I know her death was excruciating. There's her voice on the phone, consoling me just before the end: "Really, it's nothing," she says, "nothing at all. Don't cry. It's like changing clothes, that's all. It's as simple as that."

The Exile

THE BURNING STREETS of the island — he walked them, he knew them, 'til familiarity bred contempt, like the other young punks he hung out with, slept with — streets squirming with blinding heat-vapour and the furtive shadows of his brothers, white, black, what-ever, who would never get away from this island, their grotesque shadows weaving through these streets flooded in a yellow light that showed up every degrading and pathetic detail: maybe a bony dog howling in pain as it shambled across the street — beaten, tor-mented, who knows? — its lament hanging suspended in the other-wise silent air of these torpid days. Sometimes — often — a chance acquaintance, picked up in a bar or in a back-alley, might lie in the sun, in the gates of Hell, hallucinating right there on the grass, while Christopher looked on in contempt, recognizing in those hysterical, wide, unseeing eyes the reach of his own poisonous desires. He flailed against this free-fall into the drugs that were eating him up, though from time-to-time he would still wander the island, heavy-footed like some foreigner, his aggrieved shadow slid-ing along the walls. He was not himself, blind to all behind his mirror-armored sunglasses, frozen in horror or squeezed by an invisible violence he could not turn off but just hold back behind clenched teeth, teeth white and ready to tear. In California, he had been a male model, and possibly the Whites who so worshipped his body had, all of a sudden, sensed the hidden suffering that was eating its way out, for here he was, out of work on this island, with just that: his body, his beauty — the only things that might save him from the curse of his race. This guarded, mistrustful beauty and grace, which he now knew was worn and fragile under its surface splendour, made this son of soldiers — as his father had reminded him, while throwing him out of the house with his military career in ruins — into a tender and sensitive prey. He knew that here on this island they would be just as hungry for his flesh as they were in California. It would be seized and raped . . . and he gloried in this animal destiny, pliant to a hostile caress, keeping his murderous violence well hidden, deep down inside his soul. Although once, not long ago, they had lynched his kind, he would not kill them while they loved him, came on to him. That was how he wanted to live: content in his punishment, in the animal compromise he thought would lift him out of the misery, the secular burden of pain that his people had known. After all, those who have the gift of fierce beauty cannot be tamed; they appear peaceful and generous, as though put on the earth to give only love. When he walked the streets of the black ghetto (though it was said that on the island the races lived in harmony, there was still a backwater teeming with Blacks, formerly Negroes, but different from him), hands in pockets, head high and white-suited, an old woman with rotted teeth smiled at him from her balcony. This was where they lived, he thought, piled into huts, just the way white men wrote of them. Christopher answered the old woman's smile and a drunk's hello, as he guzzled beer sitting on a garbage-pile in front of his tumble-down house. Yes, he smiled at them all, broad and sly, and stroked the curly hair of the kids. Nothing seemed more affecting and vulnerable than those fuzzy-haloed angel faces, floating toward him through the thick air. "But, I'm not like them, I'm not," he thought as he crushed a revolting insect underfoot, and he thought of his father, who had said, "A career in the army could put us at the top of the black middle class." He had no use for the white man's army; he would leave them to themselves and triumph with his flesh instead . . . the flesh he had already sacrificed many times over. Unlike his father and brothers, he disliked that debonair class, the Black-American bourgeoisie, and did not want to be part of it. It was just another blemish on the history of Blacks: to get ahead in white society, you had to accept their decadence and be at ease with their crimes, while his people's blood continued to be spilled every day. His own blood would not, however; he would live purely for pleasure, but did he really feel such pleasure now, as he buckled under the heat, not having eaten for two days? Still draped in a stylish wardrobe, he hung around the expensive hotels that bathed in the reddish, twilight-glow of the ocean and waves of fire that washed over his face. He waited, but his arrogant stance told those who might have hankered for him that he was one of their own, so they barely even glanced at him. He could have resorted to those same old bars, where lust-filled eyes sparkled as soon as he walked in, but he had come here to this island for the voluptuous lifestyle of the rich. Proud and unyielding, he was not going to give in to the sweat of the impoverished, whether white or black. No, they could no longer reach him; he who had been a model in California gave off an air of nobility strolling around this island. They would know that Christopher was not one of those Negroes to be held down. He would be well off, or if he did not make it to that level of wealth he considered inelegant — and above all, he was elegant, like a panther with its claws drawn in — he would at least frequent those grand hotels by the sea, tended by magnificent waiters in airy, white uniforms over silky, pink chunks of flesh: well-muscled legs, blonde torsos, hair blown by the sweet evening breeze. He could not help admiring them; he might at least aspire to the elegant role of waiter, for there he would be surrounded by the respect and tenderness of all these blonde young men, none of them quite as handsome as he, though slightly younger. All of a sudden, he leaned against the white brick wall, dappled with sparkling reflections from the sea, and took off the sunglasses to reveal himself to those godlike creatures, light as dancers as they served the tourists. It was then, as he watched them on the illuminated terrace, young Christopher suddenly felt the weight of old wounds. He was still Christopher, but the smooth skin on which his head so often rested (and he had long lived among pushers whose flesh was just as smooth and pink, dirty little punks, nearly kids, quickly nabbed by the police, sometimes killed during a search when they fought too hard to get away . . . he always thought of them with sadness), this flesh and its smell of freedom, its perfume of wholesome, triumphant youth, these kids hanging out on their terrace — how could Christopher, unique and superior in his race, how could he fuse his dark and savage beauty with these pale creatures on whom God had bestowed the gift of daylight, while he had stepped straight out of a night of blood, a night that still clung to him like a shroud? From the depths of those eyes (under lashes as curled as the hair of the black babies he so loved holding) painfully nostalgic visions brought even more sadness to the surface, as though crystallized rage had at last begun to transform him. Maybe his flesh was tender, but so was the flesh of those pushers cooped up behind bars; even more tender was the flesh of those unharmed innocents laughing and dancing on the warmly lit terrace. Far out on the ocean, in their vast white ships, other young people were preparing for tomorrow's holocaust, there at the naval base where Christopher might have been a hero, a lieutenant like his brother Pete, perhaps . . . one of those empowered to destroy beauty and humanity. His most sacred possession, violence, still was not strong enough to draw him towards them, though, and it continued to lie dormant, unused and encased in that splendid body. In prison, there had been the pushers, really just small, unwashed boys he had held in his arms, lent his bed to (had they salvaged anything at all of that innocent candour he had tried to save . . . from a white race that corrupted itself, along with these children?). Now he no longer had anyone to stand up for. Back then in California, these same Aryan gods, called "surfers", scudded over the waves on their sailboards, weaving golden glints into beams of fire, and the sight of them had wounded Christopher's soul as well as his eyes . . . eyes lost in envy and despair behind his dark glasses. As their yachts waltzed across the water and they climbed their sky-tip-ping masts, Christopher — clad in a white suit or immaculate, white shorts — realized that though his situation was perilous, it was never going to get better. He would always be a black, male model from Los Angeles who appealed to horny old men: whether he posed nude or fully dressed, the money he made always brought bitterness and humiliation along with it. His was never going to be a conquering beauty; he was just a gorgeous slave grim-ly paying the price of his freedom by the day. Naturally inclined toward princely indolence, he would disrupt the ordered well-being that Whites had made use of for centuries, while continuing to be murderers all the while. Now that, he thought, that would be a goal worth taking risks for: to be free to haunt them with his unbridled sensuality, fearless and unfettered, while they had to live in fear and guilt with that same sensuality.

It was sunset hour on the ocean, and the island rejoiced in its birdsong and its flowering trees, while Christopher experienced a feeling of calm amid the shuddering of the earth, burning from a full day's sun. He walked across the bridge to the terrace and found himself in the midst of a group of waiters, bending to their customers with movements as fluid as if they were following the motion of the sea nearby, infused with the glow of evening. He had been watching a blue-eyed, uniformed boy from a distance, and now he heard himself asking insolently, "So, are there any jobs going around here?"

Up close, the blue-eyed, blonde-curled waiter facing him did not seem so impressive. The young man was new and had just got here from up north, but he assured Christopher, "They don't treat you right here." Already, he was moving away to throw food to the fish: it was awful the food they wasted, he said, as tourists, whispering and chuckling, watched a school of greedy fish gathering under the bridge. "Really awful," he said, eyes bright with anger. "We could feed every poor person on the island."

"But no one's poor here," Christopher said with a hint of gentleness. "Well, I'll go down to the bar and talk to the boss."

His look had hardened, though, and the blue-eyed boy could see no sympathy; standing there with an empty tray in his hand, the young man looked suddenly desolate. "Really, they don't treat us well at all," he repeated as Christopher quickly left the terrace, upset as he always was whenever he detected some sort of empathy in others. This kid was going to suffer a lot in the future, he thought, because anyone who was born white and felt compassion had to be some sort of divine being, a saint or a martyr. Christopher, whose open wounds were invisible to the naked eye, ancient, and forgotten by contemporary Whites, was also one of these earth-bound saints and martyrs. What right had this blue-eyed kid, so reluctant to do harm by throwing away food that could have fed the ghetto, what right had he to share the same privilege? Then he began to feel guilty about the snobbish way he had talked to the boy who, after all, was obviously on the side of the underdog. He had been born that way.

It was late: on his way to see the manager at the bar, Christopher could feel the warm sand running out through his sandals. This man was the personification of power; chubby and straw-hatted, he could have been one of the disgusting feeders the young boy had bowed to out there on the terrace. Christopher went straight for the man, refusing the hashish cigarette he was offered, and said he wanted to be a waiter. He trembled slightly as he said it, and his teeth shone in the night.

"Sure, kid," the man said, "we'll see. Come back tomorrow at noon. I'll be down by the pool."

At noon the next day, the torrid heat slashed like a knife through the water and the pink-and-grey roofs of the little wooden houses, so much that Christopher hesitated to go outside. Instead, he wandered through the frigid maze of hallways in the Grand Hotel, thinking about this special air the Whites had dreamed up for themselves, while outside the earth was on fire. Beneath the surface, it was even hotter: dry-burning, amid a sea of dried blood, and forgotten, but perhaps the Great Conflagration awaiting them all, would also consume those Whites, seated in their wicker chairs as they stared out to sea. Christopher's life had ended with his youth and his declining beauty, so now he could only long for that explosion in which everything, good or bad, would be consumed to ashes.

Noon, and the boss lumbered out of his green pool. He greeted Christopher naked, except for the straw hat on his baldness and a black bikini brief that spilled his fat and formless flesh, obviously a man too busy to take care of himself. "I work too hard," he said, mopping his forehead. Monster of greed that he likely was, even he played on that weakness too ready in Christopher's soul: his sympathy for Whites.

"I've come about the job," Christopher said, standing dignified before the naked man, stuck there in the sand, hat on head.

"I know, I know," he said, and Christopher shuddered from the cold hand on his shoulder. It felt like rape, this naked, ugly man, fresh out of the pool, parading his maleness and touching him. "Let's go over here."

"But that's not the terrace!" Christopher heard himself exclaim, as they headed toward the kitchens in the back. Already, he could smell the strong odour of fries.

"To start off, just do what they do, kid . . . the dishes," the boss said unctuously, "Don't worry. It'll just be temporary."

Christopher made out a row of Blacks bent over the soapy water. These were the ones you never saw in the restaurants, least of all those sunlit terraces . . . dishwashers in the stink of dead fish and grease, and he thought, "Niggers, the niggers of history, here they are." He was out of there in an instant, out of that mine of slavery and pain, with the boss calling after him, but he was gone, already out in the street, deeper and deeper into the island. Their collective soul had been beaten down yet again, same as always, same as tomorrow. "No," thought Christopher, his eyes misting as his glasses flashed blinding sunlight. "No, I won't be one of those niggers, I won't!" That was the day he lost all hope.

Voyage

HE USED TO TELL HIS daughter that they'd both be leaving soon, going way off into the country, where they'd see rivers, narrow and wide. He spoke to her like this, even if she hadn't actually become a person yet, though she did know how to read. Her name was Aline, but she wouldn't answer to it. It was a silly, little-girl name, and it weighed on her like a secret curse. Her parents knew what this curse was, but would not talk about it. They knew somehow she wasn't real, standing there in her cotton dress; yet she had a soul, a heart, and was afflicted with that same awareness they had of other people's unhappiness. That must be the curse . . . that and being able to read before she started school. Her father told her (though she knew it already) that the real people lived far away in strange countries, where they suffered, died, and were sacrificed in wars that bathed the sky in blood. He told her that, not being a real person, she was fortunate to be living here, though the apartment was too tiny and suffocating in summer, and cold in winter, because by taking even this much space for just one family, they might be depriving someone else who had none at all. In hard times like these, he said, lots of people hadn't a roof over their heads. It wasn't clear to her now whether he was talking about here or somewhere else: all their neighbours had houses, with alleys in between, even if there were rats, and babies were bitten in their cribs. There was even an epidemic of meningitis that threatened them, one after another, but still it wasn't like there, in those far-off places with their wars. They shouldn't complain, her father told her. She who wasn't anyone watched her father get up at dawn, wash and shave in front of the little kitchen mirror, and set off for the plant on his squeaky bicycle, under a low-hanging sky . . . so low it seemed to hover just over his cap and press against his pale, thin face in the first glimmer of day.

It was that time of the morning when she-who-wasn't-really-any-body stayed silent, too sad for words, not daring to tell her night-mares, too unhappy even to open the department-store catalogues in which she'd learned to read, while her mother prepared a bottle of warm milk and sugar for Kimo. It had only been a few months since her parents had brought him home from the orphanage. On his way out, her father had said, "Don't go playing with those bad kids outside any more, and take care of your brother." She would just wait till Kimo had finished swallowing that smelly mess, then take him downstairs to the yard. Even though he sometimes held on to the sticky bottle all day long, he'd started walking, though he often stopped to whimper and press his face against the legs of she-who-wasn't-really-anybody, who sometimes felt the urge to push him away. Since Kimo had shown up, with his yellowish skin and slant eyes, Aline felt as though her name, like herself, had even less substance than before, when at least she'd been able to play with the street kids down below. Sometimes, she had managed to get the better of them with her stick, when they played on the ice in winter, or when they threw stones in the deserted streets on burning-hot summer afternoons. Now, with Kimo hanging onto her skirts and whining, she was the one who got beaten. With Kimo, it was like a war, though there was no blood the way there was in her dreams. It was a thick, red, sticky blood, and it fell on the fields like rain. Here, there weren't any fields, though, just asphalt streets. There, little children were killed and fell in pieces on the fields: an arm here, a fair head there . . . the kids were all good-looking and deep in sleep under dark clouds. "You've had a nightmare. Go back to sleep," said her father, when she told him all she'd seen far away, and it was always at that moment he would tell her they'd soon go away to the country, just the two of them, and see all the rivers. Later, in that pure air, near the mountains, they would send for Kimo and her mother, and her father (one day, much, much later) would no longer work in the dangerous, smoke-filled plant that robbed men of their health and hopes. He'd have a car, maybe an old, used one: the boss — constantly in need of him — phoned him at all hours of the day or night, leaning on him, threatening him (her mother would straighten herself up proudly and say, "No, you mustn't put up with that. He's got no respect for you at all.") and the father would buckle under and obey orders, but the boss had promised him a car so he could get to-and-fro faster. "So we'll go away, travel, just us two," he would say. "Maybe we'd even have time to go trout-fishing." In the meantime, the factory weighed down on every roof in the neighbourhood, and the smoke left a greasy scum inside, a lethal dust that the mother wiped off the table every night. Dust . . . smoke . . . they ate it, they slept in it and died in it. Her father was young, thought she-who-wasn't-really-anybody; he hadn't been hurt in any war, since there hadn't been one (except between her and Kimo in the shadows of the smelly, treeless yard). So if he was young, why did he look so old when she watched him (of course, the boss had called again) lace up his shoes in the middle of the night under the glow from the electric lamp they lit late on winter nights? No, they weren't going anywhere, not to those rivers, especially the big, mysterious one with fish in summer. He was already broken and feverish, like an old man, but he was surely a real person, needed by others (like the boss who never stopped phoning, even in the

middle of the night, and brought her mother to tears at this humbling of her husband to an obedient servant). Still this was not as
bad a misfortune as they had far away: "A breakdown," he'd say. "I
have to go. Nobody else can fix those machines." It wasn't so bad,
but her mother would cry when the phone rang at night and Kimo
woke up crying, as though he were still at the orphanage, where
they'd beaten him. Then, no one could get back to sleep. With a
quick swing, her father's hat was on, and Aline knew they wouldn't
be going anywhere that day, even if it was Sunday. All of a sudden,
her father said brusquely to her, "It's not good to learn how to read
before you go to school, specially a girl." His voice, normally
patient and gentle, had become stern, and he criticized her mother
for looking at expensive things in the catalogues, things he could
never buy for her. It was selfish, he said, when people in other
countries were so badly off. Besides, they now had Kimo to feed,
too. He at least would never be an orphan again; he'd escape that
inferno. She-who-wasn't-really-anybody would listen to her father,
while turning the pages of a catalogue her mother had left open
on the table the night before. This was when she fell sad and silent,
when her father went off to the factory, with curved back and hol-
lowed cheeks, deeper and deeper, under his grey cap. Yet there
had been a time that was sadder still: at dawn, in even muddier
light, when she peeked through the bars of her bed and saw her
father up all night with his books that looked as though they had
been written in a foreign language and were filled with countless
drawings of machines, the ones he got working, and which she
hated almost as much as the far-away war machines that crushed
bodies against trees. These hostile, whining factory machines were
squeezing the life out of her father, her mother and Kimo, with
their clouds of thick, black smoke.

Then, when Sunday came around, instead of resting if the boss
didn't phone, her father went to church. On fine days, he carried
she-who-wasn't-really-anybody in the basket on his bicycle, and,
well, that would be a small trip, he said. When he let her off on the

yellowed lawn in front of the church (it seemed totally bereft of both flowers and grass) she, feeling ridiculous in her cotton dress, suddenly found herself hating this man, because he was so good, so pious and so fragile. While she hopped around outside, now on one leg, now on the other, what did he think he was going to do inside the church, on his knees in fervent meditation . . . why, pray for all those real people dying far away and whose suffering was his own secret curse! That is why, poor as they were, they had adopted Kimo : they would be rich in a love the rest of the planet was missing entirely. It was a weighty gift, this love, weightier than the burden imposed by the boss-of-the-factory-that-poisoned-them-all. If Kimo had been refused a foster home, if torture camps had opened for those of yellow skin and slant eyes like Kimo, why had they gone and taken up his war, here in a country at peace? Still, it was a peace without caring, without love, said her father when he pedalled them home, whistling with a blade of grass between his teeth, through the mean alleyways, bypassing the streets where rats bit the newborn, and veering closer, it seemed, to the highways that called on to them to take their voyage. Still, she didn't like these spots, even if her father on rare occasions whistled a sweet air, because, though there was no war, no *real* people, there was an army of little thugs who waited for her and Kimo every day with sticks and stones. That is why Kimo always had his head buried in her skirts. A little brother whose wounds were small, who wasn't a corpse in a field, Kimo didn't live far off, but right here with her in a small town where no bombs fell, and soldiers were mere ghosts headed elsewhere, not about to stay in a country where peace reigned, however heavy and sinister it may be. It was when she walked the whining Kimo through these streets that she detested her father, the goodness that brought down cruelty on his head, that had plunged them into a war of their own, a nebulous one in which she could not become anything in particular, unlike the other war, which at least made real victims, large in number and perfect in their foreignness. They need only fall and die in a landscape filled with flowers and blood, while here, people decomposed before they died. Mother, Father, Kimo, herself, they would be affected by the smoke that drifted shamefully over their houses, that corroded them all, on the asphalt that had never known flowers or blood. Then, one day, not having said a thing about the trip, the father got the car he needed for his work (only his work, the boss had said), but, yes, they just might go somewhere on Sunday. They'd see the river, the big river, at last, he told her, and this time, there would be no putting off their happiness. As usual, the boss phoned in the night, and Kimo woke up crying, but the father at least was jubilant: today the work would be a pleasure, because he had permission to take she-who-wasn't-really-anybody to a lake out in the country. For a long time, she stared at this car that resembled a long, beat-up hearse; a short while before the trip, she was afraid, but it was only her dreams that showed Kimo, lying with others far away, his slant eyes closed, so fast asleep that no amount of shaking could waken him. There was no blood in this dream, just a rain of lava . . . and Kimo, yellow, black, immobile.

It was a summer Sunday when they set out, and the father was whistling his song. For a long time they gazed at fields and forests, always at a distance, never leaving the car that looked like a hearse. She'd asked if they could stop and run through the grass, but her father said to wait until they arrived. They would soon be there, and it was so beautiful: the grass tall and stiff, and the house . . . just wait till you see it . . . paradise! She had thought the water, the sky and the trees would become real, so you could feel them with your eyes, like the letters in the catalogues. Maybe, if she breathed this air, real air, she too might become a real person, the same as her father. Still, nothing was certain, because she'd had a bad dream. Her father now wore that pale, morning face she disliked. He had laughed and sung for her, then suddenly fallen silent before the trees and sky that were no longer vibrant or tangible, the way they had been only a minute before.

They were nearing the boss' estate, his lake, his trout (which no one could fish). An iron fence separated them from the lavish gardens, ordered as though someone had sculpted them, but despite the order and tranquility, the warm air around them seemed to gel. At once, they heard dogs, and the father said, "Don't be afraid . . . they'll come close, but I know them. I often come here to fix things. I've got the keys, just like I live here." His tone was light to calm her fear. At that instant, once again, she despised the gentle, slavish goodness that made him seem cruel, for he had opened the doors of the-car-that-looked-like-a-hearse and said, as he swept aside the snarling dogs, "Go on, run all you want. It's all yours. I'll be busy for hours with the machines in the basement." Because he was a real person, of course, the dogs didn't attack him, but they nearly tore his daughter apart, so he snatched her up and put her safely back in the car that smelled like death. He was surprised to see her so timid, and she thought he, being someone, must think her cowardly. After all, a real person would have faced up to the dogs, the way he had faced up to the struggle with Kimo, the war that now surrounded their house, that was everywhere. Then, locking she-who-wasn't-really-anybody in the hearse, and blocking all openings so she wouldn't be devoured by the howling dogs he had trained to obey only him, he said, with implacable gentleness, "You're my own daughter. Why be afraid? We won't be able to take a trip again for a long time. The boss won't invite us every day." His face pressed up against the glass next to her, as he said, "Come on out and play. I'll take a break for an hour, and we'll go fishing." And she watched as his face prepared to withdraw again, far off, disappearing, as it did every morning, shadowed by his cap. She saw him and nothing else: not the lake, nor the gardens, so precisely cut . . . just that thin, pale face, the face of a forgotten victim left behind by the war, like her, and her mother and Kimo. War in a country at peace. Gradually, he faded into the distance with his tools, heading under the trees, to the house and gardens, where she could not run and play. Watched closely by the dogs, while their claws slid down the side of the car, she waited all day for this painful trip to end, a trip on which she at last realized she had become someone, someone who was going to sweep away the curse that had visited them.

Torment

AT THIS HOUR OF THE evening, when the sun set on the ocean, Gentry saw it as a thin smear of blood edging the horizon. He came and went on the uncluttered terrace, between sky and sea, inattentive to the low murmur of nearby customers, or to their vulgar laughter in the cool air of approaching night. These men and women, after drooping all day in the sun's heat, sated with food and alcohol, had already forgotten the massacres of the war years, massacres Gentry was still running from, always on the lookout for a final refuge, now in this bar which, in a few hours, would look like a deserted backyard opening onto the ocean. Who knows? Maybe one of these disgusting tourists would turn out to be a friend or a classmate from university, come here to nose out his secret and turn him in.

He smiled, put on a cool politeness, an icy fold of a smile under his dark glasses; he might pass for a waiter in his baggy shirt with red flowers, his khaki shorts — just the uniform for a waiter in these southern parts. Besides, who would really remember him from Harvard Medical School in the days when conscientious objectors went to jail? Gentry, handsome, young, and suddenly

broken, as if his backbone had given way under the whip in that
hellish prison in Peru, where he and other young drug-dealers had
thought long and hard about the war that marked them all —
whether they were pacifists like him and John, or former soldiers
like Freddy and so many more. Hadn't they all been tarred with
the same brush? Who was going to spot Gentry under his mask of
shades and his distant smile . . . a murderer or would-be murderer,
with that serene and innocent face, suntanned cheeks, and wholesome, good nature? At the neck of his red-flowered shirt there still
showed — almost indecent in these barbarous times — a few blonde
curls from other days . . . days when young men still had long hair,
though they were soon to be shaved and sent far off, bald and
broad-shouldered, many of them never to return. Suddenly, Gentry's laugh would transform into a wicked grin: they had killed
him; he was not the one who consented to his country's crimes,
who from his plane had burned straw huts and napalmed rice
fields. Yet, at night he saw little girls on fire, running; he heard
their shrieks and cries of pain in his dreams. He would sleep little,
but spend nights walking the streets; this was just about the hour it
began, at evening, when a blood-like foam glittered on the waves.
Sometimes a huge one would reach all the way up on the beach
and lie right under the terrace where Gentry could see calcinated
bodies stirring the dirty water. They filled him with terror and
shame, for he had never stopped seeing them, even when he had
sunk into a drugged stupor to forget, by the side of the road . . . in
South America . . . anywhere. He felt overwhelmed by them, as he
did by this hellish sunlight, which always seemed like the fires of
war and human destruction.

Sometimes the froth of blood distilled into a golden mist: this
was a country of despicable sweetness, he thought. Here, surrounded by this magnificence, forgetting the past and the blood
of innocents forever on the horizon, the only feeling possible was
selfish contentment. Was he really the only one of his generation
who could still sense this buried curse? Was it mostly because he

hadn't saved John from his killers in their South American jail? He had escaped, hadn't he, and left John to be tortured by the guards and finally executed with a bullet to the back of the neck. These tormentors would kill for a little stolen cocaine, and John, barely out of adolescence, was vulnerable, easy prey. It came soon after the butchery of the war, thought Gentry, and even when they'd been running free out on the highway, hadn't they seen it every-where, this troubling sun, reddening the horizon? Weren't they sure of an early death, these "flower children", ardent pacifists and conscientious objectors in search of a just peace? Gentry won-dered if there ever could be a just peace and order in such a bloody world. Hadn't they all been sacrificed, along with the other victims of the nasty war no one talked about any more?

He saw the insolent smiles of the young waitresses as they brushed against him, criss-crossing the terrace. What did they know about the hideous world they were starting out into . . . they hadn't been betrayed yet, he thought. These carefree girls would dance all night to a low-down kind of jazz and ragtime which filled Gentry with a keen nostalgia on those nights when he hung out 'til morning on the beach, not knowing what to make of his life. He saw their slender shadows high above on the brightly lit terraces that overlooked the sea: the island was swinging, though John was dead, and Gentry hadn't saved him any more than he'd helped bring an end to the war that had dragged his country through the gutter. He and John used to listen to this music; they heard in it the deafening cacophony of armaments and, far off, the bursting of bombs in the rice fields. Every evening, as families in America and elsewhere sat down to their evening meal and a diet of the morbid war-show, he'd said to John, "One day, we're gonna wipe out all these crimes," but the crimes just went on covering the earth in ashes, and their generation — candidly referred to as "flower children" — kids who passed judgement on the murders of their presidents, armies, fathers . . . at the supper table or on T.V. . . . . hadn't they committed their share of crimes too?

"Goin' out tonight, Gentry?" came these laughing voices over the evening air, as Gentry came and went, stiffly holding the tray of pink, rum-filled drinks, the same rum he secretly swigged all day long, thinning the sharp taste with soft drinks. His was a drawn-out, bitter drunkenness, and it was aggravated by the familiar sensuality of the girls around him . . . "Premature-little-old-Vietnam-guy-who-never-actually-fought," they sarcastically called him, sidling up one by one. When they turned around, he could read "Last Resort" in big black letters, as their smocks billowed in the wind. "Right," he thought. "Last stop, when there's nowhere else to go." He and John had once believed they'd found it in Peru, under that furious sun, but wasn't this really it, the end of the earth, here on this island, without him . . . surrounded by ghosts from the past? The shadows had a way of giving up all those Gentry would rather not see in the light of day: hairy young bums in winter boots, wandering onto the terrace, looking for a place to sleep it off. Freddy was one of them, a wounded hippy vet who haunted Gentry, as his wheelchair squeaked its way up the wooden ramp that seemed to have been put there just for him. On his lifeless lap, he carried a rolled-up sleeping bag tied around his neck and a heavy load of beer that disappeared, little by little, all day long, into the thin face under his cap. Gentry studied those filthy feet in their army boots, and he was sure the crippled man's pained face flashed from his mirrored glasses, as he criss-crossed the terrace with his tray and heard Freddy say every evening with rage, "If I had it to do over, I'd kill 'em all, just whip out my lighter and burn all them houses . . ."

"Shut up, you moron. That's just the crack talkin'."

"We were one sadistic bunch of mothers . . . still are. Geez, if I only had my legs . . ."

He seemed to be making a speech to those other martyrs listed in the morning papers: Dennis, William, Ivan, James, Garreth . . . all of them dead at twenty. "Died in Panama," said Freddy, waving the paper against the wind, "all of 'em in the First Batallion.

They'll get full honours. Me too, Airborne, but they got me . . . massacre, what a massacre!" he kept repeating, bewildered, and Gentry heard the lament as it rose from Freddy's body, glued to the wheelchair, and up through the sleeping bag and the beer cans. The damn war was always there, even when he thought it was forgotten. Dennis, William, Ivan, James, Garreth . . . what had they done to be sent off and killed? With what indifference had their elders, fathers, continued these crimes and sacrifices for their country? Now here he was, offering up his pink rum candies to this same generation of the rich that gorged on war. What irony, he thought: he, just as surely as John, had already given up his life for them, and they, the happy survivors, were basking in the last rays of the sun, stuffed with food and booze, without so much as a crease in their smug, fat flesh. They had survived Freddy's long-ago war, the shell-fragments in his legs, John's annihilation, Gentry's drugs . . . they had long been eating supper peacefully in front of the T.V., free of any feelings about rice fields burnt by napalm. Now there were other things to worry about: the world offered them and their children only social ills that got steadily worse. Well, they'd survive that too, wouldn't they, thought Gentry: other people's deadly sicknesses, crack, AIDS. In their own quiet way, they'd get through it all . . . and here they were, swimming happily in the island's elixirs, conquered by the sweet climate, the perfumed air. Too bad about Dennis, William, Ivan, James, Garreth, poor kids, really too bad, but they had served their country, and as for those napalm-blackened fields, don't worry about them. After all, they were finally growing flowers and vegetables in Hiroshima.

All at once, Gentry began thinking that this war, which they only mentioned with a certain shame in his hearing, might all along have been an excuse for all his failures in life; you could bum around the streets, deal drugs . . . after Vietnam and doing jail time for refusing to fight (like lots of others), nothing mattered for him and John in Mexico or Peru. God didn't love you any more, and people didn't either: no way you could have a normal life.

They all knew it when they talked about collective suicide from cell-to-cell in prison. It was the first time in history, thought Gentry, that suicide could be considered a cure for all that ravaged humanity. The fiery holocaust was everywhere, even on T.V.: Buddhist monks stoically sacrificing themselves, disappearing in flames, noble foreheads inclined amid the sheaves of fire. What were they supposed to do, wondered John and Gentry . . . follow their heroic example, start a hunger strike, jump from a fifteenth-storey window (as a friend had just done in New York) go up against the Pentagon to expose the violence by sacrificing themselves (as other pacifists were doing)? After all, what was the point in trying to live, when the world was on fire everywhere you went, and the battlefields, prisons, churches offered no comfort, or respite, or peace?

"Say, Gentry, you never did tell us which side you were on back then," Freddy needled, as he rolled his chair in the direction of the ocean, stopping at the wooden rail . . . like a dark, giant insect crawling out under the open sky, thought Gentry with a tight smile from under his shades. Every evening, Freddy and his deadbeat friends appeared — a bunch of coke- and crack-heads who'd all get caught sometime by the shore-patrol when it came by at seven with its flashlights and dogs, which it did most evenings. Gentry couldn't just chase them off the terrace, though, because they scared him with their expert brutality, their rough youth . . . and Freddy, the fallen soldier, the wounded killer, was their symbolic leader. He may not have had real military honours — probably some sordid army record, in fact. He was just an ignorant, hired killer . . . or maybe a nobody, a pitiful wreck of a kid abused by the State, a scavenger rummaging through garbage cans, like all those others Gentry had known on the road.

The waitresses weren't calling him, so he had time for a smoke behind the bar and some rum mixed with soda. The girls had noticed the rum on his breath, but he never touched drugs any more. All night long — after work, after lowering himself to wait on others, being part of their greed, watching their weariness but never sharing it — he wandered by himself, waded against the huge ocean waves, always running from what hurt so badly: John abandoned back there in a garden full of nettles, John not saved from prison in Peru — and Gentry shouting to him, "Give me your hand and jump over the wall . . . the dogs are right on our tails!" and John not showing, dragging behind, not hearing, crumpling against the wall, dead, blood all over his face.

Always at this hour of the evening, when the sun set on the ocean, Gentry saw it as a thin smear of blood edging the horizon, and he heard Freddy's sinister voice, always repeating, "You never did tell me which side you were on back then. You intellectual types, you're way too smooth and delicate for war. That's just for us poor folks, right?" And a cruel drunkenness crept over Gentry, as the slow heat from the rum began to toughen his heart, even as it awoke his senses. He contemplated the grimacing face of Freddy under its cap, and thought, Too bad he got out alive. He's got the soul of an executioner. Then he snapped, "You and your friends, beat it. Get on back to the beach. We've got to set tables for supper," knowing, just the same, they wouldn't leave. This bar opened onto the ocean, like the beaches, and it all seemed to belong to this ragged bunch. The tourists would be the ones to step aside instead. Draped in beach towels, they'd go straight back to their luxury hotels or homes under the palms; then the waitresses would be the next to leave, until Gentry saw them again at dawn, still fresh and full of laughter after a night in the discos in town. He would be drunk, staggering along with his bike, and one of them would pedal past and say, "Good night, big brother. Don't be sad," and his loneliness and a sense of perpetual desolation covering the earth would shame him.

He was thinking now there was no point in setting the tables for supper, because the wind was up, even though there was still that thin smudge of red along the horizon, and little by little, the ocean took on the colour of steel. There would be a storm tonight. He could tell from the heat and sudden winds that made one shiver anyway. These gross tourists felt the chill wind, too, and huddled against one another, then they made a run for it. Gentry actually envied the protection life gave them. They never seemed to be alone. Gentry eyed Freddy with hostility. He wasn't alone either. He actually had a family within this band of pushers and delinquents: a woman he called "Mamma" followed him everywhere, along with their three kids. Even Freddy and the other degenerates had managed to find paradise here, but for Gentry, The Last Resort was the picture of Hell. He was locked up here with no escape, he thought, surrounded by the ocean, low-hanging clouds, rough winds that threw over the chairs and tables on the terrace, and secret rum that made him sick. It had taken the place of hard drugs, still a slow death, but he didn't want to live anyway. Who knows, maybe Freddy was right: at least he'd had the courage to fight back, confront death. Maybe defending peace in a time of war was an illusion . . . oh, the old days, when he'd wanted to be pure and good — Gentry and John, conscientious objectors choosing exile and prison . . . hadn't they taken the coward's way out? It was Gentry who had got John started on drugs. Sure LSD then was just a lump of sugar that you swallowed and gave you wonderful hallucinations.

The last refuge, the last refuge, he thought, and whether it was Peru or elsewhere, he could still see John lying on the sidewalk at night, as he shook him with that faint, euphoric vigour he felt after taking drugs, "C'mon, get up, John, or you'll spend the night in jail. The place is crawling with cops, and we're screwed if you don't wake up. What you been doin' this time . . . mescaline, coke? Wake up, John," and John murmured plaintively that he was too stoned to get up. He was so weak and vulnerable, stretched out on the cement in his dusty jeans (Peru, that was it), and Gentry carried him slung on his back. He was light, and the guards were coming with dogs, first close, then all around them like a wall . . . no way out. As they were led away in handcuffs, Gentry noticed a young black man, maybe fifteen, being taken to jail, too, his profile straight and proud under the neon as they were arrested, insulted in a foreign language: what were they doing in the streets so late at night? Their passports were taken away. They had no parents or friends, and the black kid smiled at the police in proud insolence: they were going to share a cell for the night . . . no air, no water. Without them, John was going to go down first.

So long ago, and now no one remembered the man who had turned into Gentry the waiter, but Freddy and his gang were still there, laughing as raindrops soaked the terrace, Mamma's little boys running naked in the waves. "Let's bring the tables and chairs inside," yelled the chef, who suddenly appeared in his rumpled white outfit. "There's going to be a bad storm. Too bad about my Chocolate Delights tonight. I wanted to surprise the guests . . . a rose on each cake. C'mon in, Gentry. No one's going to show up. Why are you hanging around outside at a time like this?"

"It'll clear up," Gentry said, finding deliverance in the rain, as it soaked him from head to foot. He was standing there, still holding his glass of rum, caught up in feelings of jealousy. Even Armand, the expatriate French chef, had a look of relaxation he didn't like. His mane, trimmed to a punk look around his neck, and earrings repelled Gentry, but still, he could be touching with his rose-decorated cakes, his imagination, his good humour. Gentry was bitterly jealous of all that, as he was of Freddy and his Mamma, and all the others. For them, the island was a bastion of freedom. "I'm not going to waste time hanging around here," said the chef. "There's a girl waiting for me."

"Oh, you and your girls," replied Gentry enviously. "Go on. I'll close up. I like having the place to myself." Freddy and his wheelchair were headed for the beach, and Mamma was running over to him with a fisherman's raincoat to cover his head. In the torrent, the angry old hippie and his woman shared a closeness and a sensual connection (and three little wild kids, hair bleached and skins darkened by the sun, were about to pile onto Freddy's lap, which had been deadwood since the war), and Gentry thought just maybe all this heavy rain, wind and storm would wash away the red stain on the horizon — nothing else could wash away John's blood. Night fell, and Gentry's flowered shirt stuck to his chest. What an awesome rain, he thought, and his tears blew away in the wind. The chef in his wrinkled suit was leaving with a package of rose-cakes in his hand. "Women can't get enough," he said laughing, then disappeared into the downpour. What a hell of a haircut, thought Gentry, whipping off his sunglasses.

Alone, at last, he opened another bottle of rum: no need to hide, at least. Too much rain, night coming on, heavy black clouds piling up in the sky — Freddy and his bunch liked stormy nights with no shore-patrol: they'd get out their boats and gather near the port. One day, just like John and Gentry, they'd likely be hearing a voice through the fog: "We got 'em . . . Freddy's locked up." The wavering sound of the boats at anchor, a sweet atmosphere, perfumed air at night . . . it was late, and the thin smear of blood on the horizon was gone: the rain washed it all away. Time was forgiveness, and all was forgotten, even Freddy the veteran, the massacres of the war years and the faces of little girls running through the flames.

An Intimate
Death

His books are still there on the shelves, just as he left them, untouched. Some he read, and some he wrote; there are papers and notes lying on the work-table, too, because there will always be time to finish that novel or essay . . . won't there? The paintings and drawings he loved are intact as well, hanging on the wall, freshly done in orange. One is reminiscent of Gauguin: its brown bodies in sunlight an allegory of the sensuous paradise of life on an island where it is always sunny and warm. He had hung it on the orange wall just above the table, where he spends all day reading and writing. When evening comes and work is done, the laughter of his friends rises — low and heavy, even when pot-smoke has added its euphoria to the warm, night air — and just a breath of cool breeze on the back of the neck out here on the terrace and in the garden is enough to make them all a little drunk. Then, at night, you can hear him (the intellectual, once so reserved and discreet he might have seemed haughty) ambling lazily through the streets, yielding to the happy nonchalance of the island, little by little giving in to its voluptuous temptations. After all, there is time, isn't there? Later, when he no longer has to teach in that hidebound university back home, this is where he'll come to live, with his books and his friends. Then suddenly, just like that, one April morning, they have set up a hospital bed in his room, under those giant trees overarching his tropical house with their tangles of branches and leaves, and lying in pain on his bed amid the cluster of vines and entombing green, while food and air are distilled through tubes drop-by-drop into his weakened flesh, he thinks these trees should have been cut down while there was still time. They have grown so thick, so immense, they shut out the light . . . and down on the terrace, he can hear the laughter of Vic and Frank . . . and now here they are in the room, leaning over him, washing and changing him, turning him over. For weeks now they've been at his bedside. They started out by slipping a hash joint between his lips, but he refused it. He had discreetly mentioned once during a meal that spicy food no longer appealed to him . . . it burned his throat. Now in the evening air, it was time for his obligatory morphine. The hospital had been forced to fire the young male nurse who had been stealing doses from the terminal cases. He was from the black ghetto, and who knows what would become of the boy now.

Sheets of notes are spread thinly over the table, and his writing is no longer legible, the letters slanting and tortured. He can make out the misty outlines of Vic and Frank, as they cradle him in their arms to turn him over, then wash and change him like a small child. Yesterday, he got indescribable consolation from the toys they placed in his bed, then removed, because anything could injure him, even a stuffed teddy bear. His arms and legs are black-and-blue everywhere, and they cannot refresh him with a bath any more, just roll him over in bed . . . he weighs almost nothing. The slanting and tortured letters are still there among the notes on the work-table, under the painting on the wall painted orange last year, and he has enough strength to say to them with contained, helpless rage, and an incoherent rasp and a sigh — this time, they've really got to listen — "When, when will all this be over?

When will it end?" More proof that the time has come lies in the hibiscus Peter brought yesterday: the yellow flowers were about to open, but they didn't . . . shining in the light, they just refused to open. That must be the sign, he thought confusedly, the sign of his leaving. The trees are too tall in the sky, too thick: no sunlight can get through. It's usually yellow and warmish at this time of the morning. What was that he said? Frank and Vic barely heard him . . . some water? Sure, it had been hours since any of it passed his burning lips. With infinite gentleness, they raised him, helped him rest his head on the pillow. No use — it didn't help. He just kept repeating, "When will all this be over, friends. When will it be done?" He had always loved parties so much. Too bad he's not here tonight with his friends, colleagues, distant relations, all of them celebrating in this lavish old house where Frank and Vic have prepared a banquet in his honour . . . and he, who so loved parties, is somewhere else, his ashes cooling in the Gulf of Mexico. They rented a boat, David said: "You've never seen so many ashes rocked by the green water as the boat sped across it, and they were all carried away." There his trip had ended, but that night, during the banquet, the hibiscus flowered again, spreading its large, yellow corollas. Peter himself, standing next to it in quiet meditation, was the first to notice. Now it was in flower, but the one it was meant for, of course, could no longer eat or drink, much less roll over on his side to assuage his pain when asked to; he had seen it vigorous and full of life, just as his own breath grew short. The plant and Peter were the incarnation of a vital beauty he could no longer reach, even by stretching out and opening his fleshless hand. Plenty of time ahead of him . . . he could come back later to rest and write in his island home. There were more books to write . . . he'd be both editor and poet. He was going to discover new authors and show them to the world. Then, suddenly, one morning in March, there he was, the sportsman and athlete who had recently been ocean-diving, so weak he couldn't walk, being pushed in a wheelchair by a nurse at Miami Airport and all the

other airports, under the fearful and pitying eyes of a crowd whose
hostility lies barely below the surface. The man passing by is contagious, and contagion is an awful thing, especially when it feeds
prejudice, racism and hatred, he thinks, as the crowd parts for him
and he shivers with cold, even in this oppressive heat. He puts his
trembling fingers to his forehead and feels the premature wrinkles
there. The sky is warm and blue, and Vic and Frank are down there
waiting for him. Limp and weary in the morning, he allowed himself to be dressed in his blue wool sweater and grey corduroys, still
aware that the young black nurse was stealing, a little at a time, the
morphine he would be needing later on, maybe even in a few days,
who knows? Yet, limp and tired, he let them dress him for the trip.
What were they looking at under his sweater and pants, all those
people in the crowd . . . wounds, black stigmata? Nowhere had his
body been spared: he suffered as much on the inside as the outside. His breathing was laboured, his pink skin had dulled in a few
weeks, and when, just when would this hidden fire, this wind of
putrefaction die down? In the historic old house on the island,
everyone, glass in hand, celebrated him who had been handsome
and strong, vigorous and tender, the lover of life whom life had
left, the man who would never return from the Gulf, whom the
nurse had raised in his airplane seat to see the ocean as they approached, whose blue eyes had flashed with a pleasure that had
almost instantly gone out again — fixed on the green water with a
dejected intelligence. Then he sees the island, swallowed in vege-
tation, his island, and later that evening, Frank and Peter have to
admit they barely recognized him at the airport being wheeled by
the nurse. In the car, they had toured the island, seen again all
those houses and gardens he would see no more, and he had said,
"I feel a lot better already." They had covered trails, the odorous
streets of the town encircled by the ocean, and they remembered
him speaking with his eyes — yes, they were still good. His vision
was unaffected, and he was able to read and to work on his books;
his notes, with their illegible, slanting, tortured letters, were still

there in his house beneath the trees. Now, there was a banquet for him, and he wasn't there with his relations and friends, and he didn't feel the evening breeze on his neck, he didn't see the sky full of stars. Mercifully, said David, at the end, he didn't really know what was happening to him, like a small child being washed and changed . . . he, usually so proud, knew nothing of this . . . something to be thankful for. Alone, he descended into his dark distress, laughing and crying, and yet still saying, "God, when will all this be over?" and his blue eyes intelligent, wandering around the room, around his abandoned and battered body, the light of that look suddenly paralysed in the dawn light, and they all had copies of that photo where only lately one could still, for the last time, see that smouldering, blue-eyed stare in the withered, pale face. That day, he had also been wearing the grey corduroy pants and blue woollen sweater, and he had a nonchalant air as he relaxed in a red canvas chair, with his head, lightly inclined toward his hand, frail, as if about to fall. Yes, that was it, David said, as each of them looked at what was to be his farewell picture and noticed the premature lines in his forehead, the melancholy smile. Wasn't there a kind of indolence, a gentle, carefree quality, as it was when they'd smoke pot with friends, said David, or those evenings when they'd hang out in bars, or the night they met Lee, the young Japanese in a striped sweater, who skated up to the terrace-bars, hair cut very short in a fluorescent green band, glowing like a fire-fly in the night? There was a certain abandon in his smile and a grace in his hand gestures, an extreme detachment, for although he worked hard, he loved drifting too, dreaming away the seem-ingly endless summer days in a sensual numbness. Behind him in the photo is a seascape of water and sand that was so much a part of him as he posed with it, relaxed, ready to break out into his booming laugh, there in the garden, in the red chair his friends had given him . . . writers from all over the world . . . then it was the hospital bed in his room, and he noticed how tall and leafy the trees stretched to the sky. No, there was no sunlight or air coming in, and the hibiscus Peter had placed next to his bed, its yellow flowers had suddenly been arrested, as though shrouded in gelatin or deprived of the sun. Worn down by those base, humbling sufferings he had felt that same night, when he had told his friends he no longer liked spicy food, the lightness of his smile had disappeared, cool water no longer passed his burning lips, and a rotting fire was burning at his heart and his insides. The wasted body was barely visible under trembling, damp sheets. Though Vic changed them constantly, they were never dry. Oh, when would all this be over? Finally, at dawn, the glimmer of fierce disquiet settled into his eyes, the hibiscus stopped flowering . . . it was over.

The boats continued to glide over the green waters, and when the wind blew too strong, young surfers were thrown up by the waves; a cold breeze slid over the water, and for two days, the flower did nothing. The wind cut like a knife, and a young man died still full of the stuff of life, his books and writing still intact on the shelves and on his table, with the piles of bills still sealed in their envelopes, and that night, they celebrated him. He had ceased to feel the chill breeze on his neck, Lee no longer came at night on his skates with a fluorescent green stripe on his prickly head . . . and they drank a toast to the lover of parties.

The Sacred
Travellers

⸺ ⁓ ⸺

FIRST INSTANT
first movement: allegro vivace

POISED ADMIRABLY, not yet at their highest, hands waited, as in a dream, for the orchestra's supple return of suspended harmony. Scarcely perceptible, fingers trembled over piano keys, perhaps already floating on the silence of hidden rivers, gliding over waves real enough to touch.

These thoughts were Miguel's, as he sat by his wife, Montserrat, in the Parisian concert hall. One of many witnesses to the music, a traveller from reality, quietly resting a moment on this Sunday, May 3. He loved this Mozart concerto.

It was four o'clock, and Miguel was in a twilight of his own, dark as the sun which, at that very moment, was making shadows from the long vault-stones in cathedrals all over France. It was on Tuesday and Wednesday that he and Montserrat had beheld these worlds of night.

"This week seems to be going by so slowly," Montserrat had said, as they passed under the portals of fire and ashes. "I'm tired." Her

breathing had been too slow, and Miguel was disturbed: it had tor-
mented him, as it did that morning when she'd shot him an impatient smile at the stairs of a house in Spain . . . a fixed, embattled
smile, full of shadows. From time-to-time, Montserrat took on that
indefinable age that so brutally left its mark on her. It was then she
began breathing rapidly, believing it would dissolve a wave of
anger or *ennui*. Miguel was fearful of extreme passions: Montserrat
knew how to reveal them with a single breath.

"Miguel, my love, today's Sunday."

Now, though, she said nothing. She just listened and watched
the hands of the young pianist, as they wandered in distant, limpid
circles that only she could see. This was a face she had sculpted,
the hands too, in marble or stone or wood . . . was it Thursday,
Friday, Saturday? She closed her eyes.

Miguel sensed this and knew she had done it to be alone with
herself, subject to the violent night of her soul. Thus she could
marshall her memories with a finer understanding.

Montserrat. Montserrat.

He used her name like a probe, to see how far below the surface
she was sinking. Oh, to grasp such a fugitive love!

Miguel. Miguel.

"You must stay away from me, Johann."

She had sculpted that face in wood on Wednesday, Thursday
and Friday. Yes, that was it. His look, above all, had penetrated her
with a pained and fleeting grace; then she had covered up his
uncertain, splendid features.

"You must stay away from me, Johann."

"Johann has to return to Italy for the Venice Festival on Sunday.
He's expected. Will you go as well, Montserrat?"

"I shall stay with Miguel in Paris."

Voices, known and unknown, awakened in her mind.

"Tonight, I'll sleep better," she thought *(she paid no more attention
to the hands of Johann, which played only for her)*. "Yes, what a sleep, eh
Miguel? Like that heavy sleep in Spain, when we woke up, naked

and far out, on a pier that was so wonderfully pale."

This Sunday was Johann's moment of glory, the same glory that had abandoned Miguel the previous Sunday . . . at the very same instant. A profound happiness would always separate them: "Why you, Johann, and not me? Why are you the chosen one?"

"At last, tonight, I shall sleep," thought Montserrat.

She remembered perfectly last Sunday and the disastrous opening of Miguel's play. He was devastated. Maybe that was when he lost faith, and not on Monday in the cathedral at Chartres.

She opened her eyes.

Johann awaited the orchestra, his head bowed above the vast, inanimate hands.

This was how she had quickly sketched his face on an old binder, before daring to slant that forehead in wood on Sunday, yes, Sunday . . . the same day as Miguel's failure?

"Montserrat, Montserrat," said Miguel without looking at her, all through the First Movement . . .

Sunday . . .

Sunday

WHY WAS IT THE young poet wrote a story about misunderstood angels, and why this particular Last Judgement? No one knows. What goes through the mind of a clumsy, yet moving director who thinks he can bring life to his characters, when suddenly they slide away and metamorphose into slippery, ironic ghosts? How does he create that pain, slowly rising from the depths of time? Where does he find the nerve to bring it to life outside himself? Miguel, tell me . . . I so much want to know.

These thoughts were Johann's, as he sat next to Montserrat, his lover, in the Parisian theatre. He adored the play. His passionate attachment to it was irresistible, but the rest of the audience didn't want to face this new torment . . . the torture of Miguel's soul, a man thus far unknown to them. The crowd was weary, not wanting to suffer or to rebel any more. What did they care about judging winners or losers? To their minds, God had long since ceased to exist. Miguel, a young man alone, continued to battle the shadows, stepping into the actors' night — their muffled backstage — both master and slave to the absolute inspiration he saw pooling around him like the lament of an awkward *ingenue,* recognizing with endless repetition the cry of his own liberated heart in every line that was delivered, with each breath, under the tomb of every silence, and painted on the masks of every character.

Yet Miguel knew well his tragedy was a mistake. He was taking part in the birth of a blunder. Now, courageously, he could wait for the resounding failure of this poem, at once both as brief and as long as life itself. There was nothing more to be afraid of.

It was four o'clock, and Johann entered the dying day, dark as the body he had embraced at night and whose passionate glow still lived in him. "This week is too short," Montserrat said, caressing his hair.

"You don't love your husband?"

"Oh, I love him. I love him violently. You have to keep away from me. Damn me . . . your face has been following me since the day I was born. I'll never be able to resist you."

"I've never known so much," he said.

"You were barely a young man, not yet sixteen, when I saw you play a Mozart concerto in Vienna, and I fell in love with you forever."

"That year *(it was just after a war; I wanted to feel myself on another plane)* I played that same concerto in Austria. I met young musicians, conductors and composers from all over the world. One of them was the girl I married."

"Why didn't she come to Paris with you?"

"She's expecting our second child."

"Let's not talk any more," Montserrat replied.

It was still only the first act, and Miguel was anxious for silence. When would it be over?

Montserrat, Johann — the two beings he loved most in all the world. He could see they were born to be where they were at this moment — harsh, triumphant, bruised, and innocently perused by Miguel's banished soul. Johann, Montserrat . . . they were springing to life just as he was approaching death. Why had she introduced them on Saturday? Why had she invited Johann to have champagne with them that same Saturday . . . why?

"Darling, here's someone I've been waiting to introduce to you. I know you'll like him. You really shouldn't be alone."

"But I'm not alone. I'm with you."

On Saturday, Montserrat had been sculpting the bust, and that was when he saw him for the first time. Johann Van Smeeden. Miguel cursed his overactive memory. It was like a play on a set too lavish . . . Montserrat raising a cup to her lips with a languid gesture that encircled Johann's silhouette; Miguel alone noticed the invisible embrace, connected as he was to all that was around him. Montserrat threw her head back and drank slowly, while showing her teeth. This new lover was a woman glowing with joy as it sprang from a fresh new body.

"I'm sorry, Johann, but you really shouldn't leave on Sunday . . . or perhaps you need to go back to Venice for a rest?"

"More than a rest, Ma'am."

"Don't say it. I don't want to know."

"I have a lot of friends waiting. Couldn't you be one of them?"

"No, I can't. On Sunday, Miguel wants to return to Spain. We haven't seen it in . . . how long, Miguel?"

"A long time," he replied.

"We aren't going to let you go."

She gave a bored laugh. Miguel saw it, with her right hand to her lips. No, that wasn't it. She was stifling her surprise, something she mustn't say. Montserrat never laughed from boredom. Suddenly, Miguel found himself moving, then standing next to her.

"Montserrat, are you thirsty?"

"Just a little."

He sees himself fill the glass, then present it to her gloved hand. She is wearing a velvet dress with pleats to the knee, her smooth legs faintly coloured like fruit.

"Miguel never drinks. He works a great deal. He needs me to tell him when it's past midnight. If he wants to return to Spain, that's what we'll do."

A look from Johann cuts short the invisible embrace.

"No, you must keep away from me."

"You know I've got to go home on Sunday."

Thus the motionless lovers were separated. Johann said something about springtime in Paris, the odd freshness of the girls there. "There is an all-encompassing hope in their eyes," he said.

"What hope do you mean?"

"You could never know," he said, downcast.

"But my husband knows all kinds of things and tells me the instant they come to him," Montserrat said.

"I feel awful like this with you," said Johann, "I can't begin to understand you."

Montserrat tilted her head, smiling, "But we're all right, aren't we?"

Her hand was shaking and she forgot about her champagne. Her knees trembled imperceptibly. Miguel caressed her shoulder fondly. "It's nothing," he said, "don't let it bother you."

She came around and held herself upright, maintaining a delicate balance. "This young man wants to shake us."

"You're right, Montserrat."

"We've never been sad," she began again, as though consoling a child (and this child was the poor creature inside, never to be born), "have we, Miguel?"

"Never," he said.

Then Miguel had used the guise of amazement to change the subject: "How do you go about playing a concerto?" he asked. "It's always mystified me."

"Tell us the truth," Montserrat said (her voice no longer trembling, *now serene).* "We're passionate people, the two of us. Miguel won't learn self-control. He has set in motion an astonishing sort of machine they call a 'production'. I've seen this up close, at dress rehearsal. I was flabbergasted. Miguel is astonishing, fantastic even, but he doesn't know anything," she said *(slowly, very slowly, she was speaking only for Johann now, Miguel having stepped away momentarily to close the blinds).* "He doesn't know things, because he allows himself to be torn up by whatever moves him. I don't really know him. Don't listen that way, Johann. You'd get to know my husband better on your own. You'll see. It's like those sandcastles he used to build next to me when we were in Spain. Everything he creates or writes is threatened with extinction like that."

"I feel sorry for him. I really do," said Johann.

"He wishes he could feel sorry for you too," Montserrat said. She took Johann's hand and, speaking softly, murmured, "Oh, you rejoice in being immortal!"

"No, you must understand . . ."

Miguel was coming toward them, and they fell silent. He sat next to Montserrat: "I felt a sudden heat," he said.

"The flames that rise within one at a moment's notice take getting used to," replied Montserrat, then nothing more.

The silence weighed on Miguel, not knowing how to end the first act of his tragedy. A man, himself, was addressing the audience directly. Johann and Montserrat seemed to be only half-listening, their faces breathtakingly fused into one.

"Saturday was when I saw you for the first time, Johann. I'm not quite sure what I felt at that moment. My wife loved you. During the night, you had taken her. Yet there you were before me, free of anger or hatred, as I was before you. Montserrat was basking in your innocence. You were conscious of not wanting to hide your love of Montserrat from me, and I the same . . . enemies and equals. What was it about you that tore into me the moment I first saw you?" . . . Keep him away from me, Miguel mused.

"Montserrat was chiselling your features in wood. There you

were, a little remote, especially from yourself, detached from those movements that were making you into a model, or rather a victim . . . I'm not sure which . . . Montserrat's movements, which held you, even then. You were the captive of an unknown twilight. How Montserrat must have loved you to want to imprison herself in this perishable model! Were you . . . are you mortal, though? I have felt the chaste burden of immortality weighing down on your head.

"I was drawn to you then, as thunder to silence, or night unable to resist day — its end and its purpose — but not as a woman is to a lover . . . more than that, beyond death, into the vacuum created by the breath of angels. You were the Angel of Light, the tempting angel come to save or damn me. That you were.

"Tireless and silent, my wife's hands tamed your features wonderfully, but were they able to reach that light, that wild transparency? Montserrat drew out your face at the cost of her own inner shadows. 'I've never seen anyone as immobile as you are, Johann,' she said smiling. I took the measure of her abysses from that breath of burning anxiety, close to regret, even remorse. Who could help but notice that despairing way of turning inward?"

"Don't you ever smile, then, Johann?" said Montserrat.

"One day, we'll be able to without wreaking destruction around us, don't you think?"

"No," she answered, stiffening before her sculpture, but prepared to bend before the man.

"Talk to us . . . to me," Miguel wanted to say. "No, I wouldn't dare ask you. We'd been tossed out of Paradise."

"Strange," said Montserrat, "Miguel believes strongly in God, but will he tomorrow or the next day? Your indifference was perhaps that which lies beneath the depths of an inaccessible sort of love. Your presence, sharp and yet extremely gentle, evoked in me a world without name: a hope, the meaning of which is now lost to me. This Angel of Light is to blame for suddenly opening the Oceans of the Supernatural before you."

"Be quiet, Johann," Montserrat suddenly interjected, "Really, you must be quiet! I must be in peace to do my work. Never has a young man made things so difficult before, though I've been touched by lots of different faces. You're just a man like any other. Still, there are days when life turns strange, and nothing is what it was before. Don't you agree?"

"Yes," Johann said without lowering his eyes, "I actually lead a very simple, normal life with my wife and our child in Vienna, too distant from music to deserve being its intimate interpreter. I've never seen a life as limited as mine," he added.

An hour later, as Montserrat seemed tired and in need of solitude *(I always know the moment this solitude becomes essential and urgent)*, I asked you to follow me to the studio, so you could get to know her work.

"Temptation", that was the first piece we saw together. It seemed to incarnate Johann's being, a lightning-bolt of revelation at the edge of our lives.

"Temptation," said Johann, "why does the young man let himself get drunk on shadows? Isn't he reaching out to them?"

"No," I said, "he's surrounded by light."

"That face of terror," he said, "he has no idea where he's headed."

"His expression is pure. It already sees the future."

"Who is that demonic young man?"

"Why demonic? He's not young, or even a man, but something else. How could such a race of beings be diabolical? Does Satan himself exist?"

"I think your wife can't stop herself," he said, "from giving birth to the devil in this sculpture."

"Ghosts."

"Souls," said Johann, "still more souls . . . and perhaps a body . . . bodies moving toward the darkness, wise souls but hopeless ones," he added, "countless bodies."

"Yes, numberless. Montserrat said she saw them walking through the night. I wasn't there. I knew nothing about it."

"Why are some of the bodies so young? Here, this one's just a child."

"You know, I never noticed before."

"The Young Girl of Sleep."

Simply the bust of a little girl, Montserrat herself, maybe.

"Dead?" asked Johann.

"No one knows," I replied.

"Sleeping in the cleft of a dream," he suggested. "I like that straight neck and its clear light . . ."

". . . and the eyes?"

"Let's not talk about them," Johann answered.

At that point, Montserrat came in. She walked up to me and took me by the arm. "Why did you leave me all by myself? I fell asleep."

"You've had too much champagne."

"I feel as though I've awakened from the dead," she said. "Quite reassuring, really." She lowered her eyes, then stopped in front of the bust of of the little girl. "That'll do, Johann. Don't try to understand. You must go easy on me." Then, turning to me, "Why did you do this, Miguel? You know I don't like showing off my work."

"But it has such rich emotions," said Johann.

"It is life, that's all," said Montserrat, "and mine is of little consequence. Come away, my friends. Come on." This time, she took us both by the arm, walking between us, lightly following our steps.

Montserrat and Johann were still attentive, as the first act ended, and Miguel fell silent.

INTERLUDE

"I ought to talk to Miguel and reassure him. He is suffering in secret."

"No, don't go," said Johann, "you've been crying. He'll see. Let's just wait. The second act's going to begin. Who knows, maybe it will bring him peace?"

"Strange," Montserrat said, "people aren't getting up."

"Let's go out for a minute," Johann replied. The Paris evening is bright. I want to see it with you."

Johann put his arm around her shoulder. Long and slender, his body seemed to lift Montserrat as they walked. Yesterday she had left everything in her wake, but now she seemed adrift, like a fallen leaf.

"It's raining," she said, "That'll do me good. It rained for forty days and nights in Paris, but the fire in Miguel and me never wavered a second. Endless suffocation," she added, tilting her head downward.

"The Little Girl bust," Johann said. "I can still see it. She isn't dead."

They had already begun to embrace and were nearly finished, silently surrounded by the spring storm. Johann kissed Montserrat and held her against the wall. "What do you want with me?" she asked him *(torment raced briefly through her deep eyes)*. "Stay away. I mean it. Stay away from me."

"Let's walk to Notre Dame."

"No, we've got to go back in. Miguel's alone, and he's waiting for us."

He started to release her.

"No, don't leave me," she said.

He pressed her to him again.

"I don't know what is in your heart. That's what hurts most."

The rain dropped onto Johann's eyelids and ran down his solitary lips.

"Bronze man," laughed Montserrat. "It's absurd . . . I love you, O man in the body of the sun."

The rain glistened on Montserrat's cheeks, as though water could rekindle ashes. Their beauty had the clarity of dark objects suddenly plunged into brilliant daylight.

"There's going to be another downpour," Johann said, "but you'll make it."

"I'm happy," she answered, "happy because Miguel is here too."

They were now on their way back to the theatre. This moment, like an oasis, had softened Montserrat's laughter. "You laugh so awfully and so wonderfully," Johann remarked.

"I was so taken with you out by the piers that I forgot to look at the Seine."

"You also forgot to watch the people running to get out of the rain, the Paris crowd: women and kids."

"Oh, well, excuse me! I had eyes and ears only for you. I even started to forget that Miguel was waiting back at the theatre."

"They jumped into the Seine," said Johann.

"Who did?"

"What did you say? I can't hear."

"That's right. There have always been wrecks in the Seine."

"Let's walk faster," he said.

"But I'm running already."

"We mustn't be late."

"I've really been rushing."

"We've got to get there in time. We'll never make it. Come on," he said as Montserrat's waist bent to his hand, like an animal leaning into a murderer's caress. And then, "No, you mustn't think of me as your enemy!"

"It's true, then. The devil does exist," shouted Montserrat.

(She knew that already, though, and was denying everything she had lived through up to now, all for the hand at her waist . . . holding her over the void. Appalled, she tasted this tearing caress, and a darting flash split her peaceful expression.)

It isn't he who is the seducer — it's me, she thought. That's right. I asked you to be my lover. I'd never been unfaithful before. It changed nothing about my love for him. "Demon," she said *(she said it softly, and Johann heard a sound like sobbing),* not just the demon of infidelity, but that other one that tries to convince us it was created by God, the Son of God, as I am a daughter of the earth and wife to Miguel. "Darling, be a man, no more than that, I beg you: a few more nights with me, and you will be as material as every other living thing in the world."

"Quiet," said Johann, "the lights are up. Follow me."

"In Vienna, the first time I saw you, I finally realized who you were: that candid, wild young pianist."

"It's the second act."

While they remembered *(they had been doing it for a while, but the Earth had aged considerably in that time, and men had faithfully continued to die with each second, so the thoughts of Miguel and Montserrat could triumph on this Sunday in May, and give motion to the planets before the seventh-day rest that was approaching)*, faithfully, too, Johann's hands gave life. It was the second movement of the concerto: andantino.

When she saw him enter the brown-coloured room *(she had lit some lamps, but little by little they went out, from yellow or pink to brown, like Montserrat's hair — she could no longer pin down the ecstasy in a colour — the smell of a Paris evening, like a damp bird rising from each street after the storm, wafted in through the shutters)*, she felt drunk with the idea that he was in her room, like the chance breeze that stirs an infertile season, tragic as the wind — yes, it was — and as unkempt as himself, he came to her.

"Montserrat, Montserrat, how did it happen to be you?"

"I won't know unless you tell me."

She did not get up. Stretched out on the bed, with her arms crossed and her feet tied down by night, she waited for the face, the eyes. Slowly, he knelt over her and then waited.

"Where am I?" she asked.

"It's raining heavily outside," he said. "Can you hear me?"

"No," she replied.

"We had a downpour just like this, last month in Vienna."

She threw back her head.

"You sometimes wear white dresses, don't you?"

"When I was a little girl, I had white shoes. I ran through the snow and the sand with Miguel. One day, he pricked my finger with a thorn. The blood ran into the palm of my hand. That's when I became his fiancée. We've often become engaged . . . in the brambles, in summer and winter, especially in summer. I'll do it again. I do love him."

"Yes," said Johann, "you do."

"It's always been our destiny."

"Under your green dress, your dress . . . blue or green *(Montserrat laughed tenderly. He always got it wrong, leaning over this body that had been granted to him, better than ever, because he had not yet possessed it).*

"Red, my dress is red."

"Under your red dress, what colour would your body be tonight?" He undressed her and drew his arm across her hips.

"Don't stretch your arm out towards the infinite. Just draw a line with your soul, like those I saw. Those souls, walking into the night, countless, more numerous than the stars," said Montserrat. "This is a poem my husband wrote." She sighed, "Now that I'm naked, am I newborn? Are you judging me?"

"We're together," he said, "and you are beautiful and dark. Your body is in full rebellion." *(Yes, in rebellion against all that dies, thought Montserrat.)*

Night had fallen completely, and Montserrat let her hands and feet be loosed. She had just dressed and lain down beside Johann, the sleeper she loved more than sleep itself, so much had she longed to know this man and the repose that made him even more irresistibly human.

"I'd always taken you for a man . . . no more, and it's enough to know he is in you. Perhaps Miguel believes God exists, and you too, Johann, but I'm safe from God and from you. I'll go on trying to discover who you are, so I can be the most human prey possible to you. It's not Satan I'm being unfaithful with, just a man . . . Johann Van Smeeden, a musician I met in Vienna, now in Paris to play a Mozart concerto. Whoever you are, you tempt me, and I've sought you out since the day I was born."

Johann took her hand: "Who did this . . . made your finger bleed?" he said. "What thorn and what childhood fiancé?"

"Sleep a little longer," she said. "I was thinking . . . still am, and chewed my finger without realizing it. The edge of my tooth did that. You can go to sleep now, Johann. I think about everything."

She went into Miguel's room: "It's dawn, Miguel, we have to stay up for the dress rehearsal. I promised to come, and I will. What's the matter?"

"There is an angel in the house."

"Are you sure that's what it is?" she replied.

She raised her husband's head: "Darling, we're still young, and perhaps other times lie ahead for us, better, sweeter times, like our childhood in Spain. Come on, get up. Who knows what's going to happen next?"

"Is it still raining out?"

"I never wear a blue dress when it does. You know that."

"It's green," he laughed. "You always get it wrong."

"Yes, it's raining, Miguel."

She was in a hurry to forget: "How mysterious you are; how drawn to you I am! Of course, we'll go wherever you like."

How could we ever go back to Spain, though? *(She had mentioned the lost shoes to Johann. All of a sudden, she'd remembered.)* Let's go to Rome . . . or Greece, love, the way we used to. Oh, why do you always write such great sadness?

Is that it . . . the end of the tragedy? Just like that?

The audience remained seated, motionless in the shadows . . . feeling merely ironic, not at all amazed. These humdrum enemies expected nothing of anger and hate any more.

The curtain came down. Miguel heard a cry from his inner depths, and he drowned.

He had been wrong. There had been no resurrection. After this patient unfolding of words and scenes, the tragedy had left behind only a pathetic cry, one he knew from the day he was born, but no one else heard it.

"Get up, Montserrat. Go over there. He needs you. Go to him."

"This is insane," she said. "I don't want to. Don't you think I know when he's in pain? I love Miguel."

"You've got to be with him . . . right now," Johann pleaded.

Montserrat sank deep into her seat and did not get up.

Monday

ON THE TRAIN TAKING them to Chartres, Miguel and Montserrat fled the ravenous rains that devoured Paris. Occasionally Miguel's face would plunge brusquely into the dawn and soak up a patch of gold that saddened his brow. Bathed in a fleeting peace, he drew away from Montserrat's hand, even as it sought his wrist.

"What is there to complain about, Miguel? We're together. We'll see Paradise, then leave it all behind us. A great deal was promised to us, long ago in Spain, before we were old enough to know . . . old enough to know about pain that was aware of itself. How is it I've forgotten all they promised us when we were born? I wanted to be earth, life . . . as simple as that. Why are you unhappy? *(Her voice was urgent and warm, like one filled with love.)* We've been around the world together, looking for what we'll never find. We could have been separate and alone, but here you are, and I beside you. We thought Paris was beautiful when we were twenty, because we were in love. How can you be so ungrateful toward us? Yes, us two."

He smiled at her and said, as if in a dream, "When I was alone in Rome without you, what pain I felt. You'll never know the times I thought of you . . . in streets or gardens . . . next to fountains. That sun I looked at with your eyes, you'll never see it again with me."

"Do you really think I didn't know all that?" she asked.

"Oh, you don't. Love knows nothing," he answered. "Are all these people going to Chartres as well?"

Absently, she replied, "I have never known anyone as blind as you!"

"I think I know who you are," said a girl suddenly. "Didn't I see both of you in Vienna in October?

"Maybe," said Montserrat.

"What's your name?" Miguel asked.

"Vinca," the girl answered, "Vinca Van Smeeden. My fiancé will be here in a moment. I'll introduce you. No, wait, you already know him. He's just in the next compartment, talking to the kids. We have a concert tonight in Chartres. These rowdy young people around us *(Montserrat shuddered, not having heard any of it yet)* are members of our orchestra. My husband's collected them from all over the world. They're still too young to be perfect musicians, but my husband is the conductor, and he has confidence in them."

Montserrat had submitted to these very words somewhere before. She didn't know what time or day, but she was as sure as *déjà vu*.

"What about yourself?" asked Miguel.

"I'm a pianist," replied the girl. "Tonight, I'm playing the Mozart concerto."

She crossed her hands on her knees.

"You seem very relaxed," said Montserrat. "I'm sure everything will go fine for you tonight."

"The orchestra received a good reception in Rome, and this past summer in Greece, too. Soon we'll be going to Venice."

"Venice," said Miguel. "We've heard so much about it, but my wife and I won't be going there."

"John, you remember our friends from Vienna, don't you?"

"I met Madame for the first time in Austria," the young man said.

He stood motionless before his fiancée, glancing sideways at her, while Miguel struggled with his thoughts.

"Come on, Miguel," said Montserrat. "Why wouldn't they look alike? There are lots of them on the planet. They are a race, Miguel, a splendid race!"

The young man sat down next to the girl. In the narrow corridors of the train, young people were leaning out of open windows, light as doves in a seascape.

Montserrat returned to Miguel's hurt: "He says he doesn't believe in God, not any more, but bit-by-bit he's discovering a new one . . . the ultimate one that exists only for a moment, at the instant of death. It's the god of imagination. Be strong, Miguel."

The cathedral at Chartres began to take form out of the fog.

"John, oh John, look at the sun on that stone!"

"Tell me about the sun," Miguel urged.

The young man didn't answer, and Montserrat's indifferent ears caught the laughter of the children.

Chartres

"THIS ANDANTINO," THOUGHT Miguel, "Johann plays the world and time, and infinity surges from those gulfs of harmony. Infinity is merely the release of joy, after all. Johann holds the secret to the human adventure at last. He knows what I cannot know . . . and never will."

Montserrat. Montserrat.

By her side like this, she knows he is seeking her out at the world's core.

Montserrat. Montserrat.

We saw the century writ on every stone, every door, every steeple.

He entered the nave by one of those timeless doors.

Then, suddenly, he disappeared.

How could that be? We had no inkling.

Miguel. Miguel.

A woman leaned in the tallest doorway.

Forever with child, she was never to become a mother, just the blessed, humble form of Innocence.

(An unknown hand had shaped her heart from the bark of France's trees. The setting sun had set it ablaze so often, but it beat always, gentle and vulnerable.)

Notre-Dame-Sous-Terre.

At Notre-Dame-Sous-Terre, I lost her.

In a murky chapel, dogged by the mist. Miguel. Miguel.

"She holds her child on her knee, the Virgin who must give birth. Would you like a child, Montserrat?"

"No."

"But why, Montserrat?"

" Despite myself, my body would still be intact."

". . . and chaste?"

"Yes."

I walk in mist. What do you expect?

What do you expect, Miguel?

I'm thirsty for the well of Saints-Forts.

He was thirsty.

Peoples long extinct have drunk at this sacred well.

You, Miguel?

I'm thirsty.

People thronged here in the eleventh century, wanting to cure the wound of their humanity.

One drop of this holy water, Miguel.

My thirst goes back to yesterday, to the moment you were born, to before you and after you, Montserrat.

In the ninth century, they came here in droves to be cured.

Humanity's dream.

They came, and still I am thirsty. Why is that?

They built a cathedral facing east, and another . . . to protect the first, ramparts rearing in the night.

Long ago.

I am listening, Miguel. I hear you, but the mist shrouds me.

Your beloved face.

To the east was built a glorious country.

"August 5, 962 A.D., the dawn fire . . ."

"No, that was September 7 or 8, 1020 . . ."

"And again, soon afterwards, on May 3."

Clothed in spray and nothingness, he crossed two long, parallel galleries, one to the north, and one to the south. He fled and vanished under the vaults.

Miguel. Miguel.

"See that steeple surveying our loneliness."

In the deep shadows of the steeples, Miguel walked without ever knowing that the gigantic statues held prisoner against the doorways, reassured him with their mysterious presence.

He entered the temple.

They watched like sisters from another age, wistfully, perhaps, their marble eyes full of thought, but reflecting nothing . . .

Prisoners of respect.

On each portal, the word for the sculpture, triumphant —

The Son of God ascends to heaven.

Listen, Miguel. Look, Miguel,

But he wasn't watching.

An old man at the Apocalypse, his face — a curse on me —

I'll not forget it,

Terrible guardian of the evening.

Miguel wasn't looking. He was walking far off.

"Angels . . . and more angels in those curves," Miguel said.

"They must exist too, Miguel."

"The Saviour's life unfolded in the windows, least known of the Passions."

"What are you thinking about, Miguel? May I know?"

"No," he said, "too late."

Next, I saw a row of horses,

Docile, they'd barely quit this life.

When I found Miguel he was lying on a tomb of stone. I saw no more fog.

The newly risen sun bathed his feet and his hands. Like the blood of the day that had not yet acknowledged its wounds.

"It's so warm and beautiful!" he said.

Handsome sleeper, do you know who I am?

No woman knew him as I did.

Or misunderstood him as I did.

(I recall that sculpture I'd finished in Paris a few days before. "The Hope of a Weary Young Man." Miguel was the inspiration for it. I was discovering him. The arm around an unknown form, the abstract offering of a sigh . . .)

"Come closer," Miguel said. "Tell me where you were."

"In the crypt," replied Montserrat.

She took off her shoes and came closer. Majestic and simple, she approached like a floating line on the water.

The voice said, "Montserrat, where were you?"

"Looking at that Madonna made me remember our childhood. Alone with her black tears, then as now."

"What are you talking about?"

"Nothing."

"Come," said Miguel.

I lay down next to him on the tomb at the foot of the cathedral at Chartres and wrapped myself around him.

A morning in April, or May, or December? Who knows? "Tell me, my love. Teach me."

"For he taught me everything when we were children: how to love a bunch of grapes spilling from their basket, the shadow forming under our feet . . . our sandals, when we ran, how to jump from a horse without getting giddy. We leaped into every space, we two."

"I love you now and in the time to come."

"Say it once more."

"One man loves you, and it is me. Silence within you, Mont-serrat."

And space was a rose.

We walked in the summer perfumes, he and I.

Our blue cloaks kept out the winter cloudbursts.

"Teach me how I must live."

"I'm afraid I'm very weak," she said. "I'm afraid I've grown very old."

"Life creates itself as you go on loving me."

"Life, yes . . . and I'm not as weary as I'll be tomorrow."

"Silence within you, Montserrat. I'm looking for you at the earth's core."

"Life creates itself as you go on loving me."

"Yes, it is life, isn't it? After all, I'm only a little the worse for wear. You see," said Miguel, "I'm still here."

"But not the same any more," she said brutally.

(Lost, he contemplated this dark innocence with a changing eye.)

"In you, I shall love many thousands of others."

"To the end of the world, if you are faithful," said Miguel.

"Perhaps I am faithful," she replied.

Little by little, they took on the colour of the stones, narrow sculptures of spring under a bursting sky.

Monday: night-time . . .

DEAR SOUL,

(She shivered and remembered that she had wanted to be just the enchanted illusion of a body for him — mere trappings of a great and lofty passion.) All day, my friends and I have been working at the Opéra in a damp rehearsal hall.

This humidity was coming from Paris awash, cooled by the rising moisture of the fog, climbing about me like a wounded animal.

"What are you doing?"

"I was reading a letter, Miguel, from abroad. What about you, iguel. Where were you?"

"Listening to a Beethoven concerto."

"Today at Chartres is getting to you, isn't it?"

"How to explain all that I've understood and lost in a single day, ontserrat?"

"I know, Miguel. Say nothing."

"Where are you going in that raincoat? Can't I go with you?"

"Rest, Miguel. I'm simply going to walk to the Opéra. Then I'll me back at night and go to sleep with you."

"We always have to be saying goodbye, don't we?"

"Yes."

Andantino. It is a long movement, full of contrasts. Play, Johann. ie planets are alive . . . Play, Johann. Everything is immortal, and thing that has been will ever be forgotten.

Those admirable hands, still not fully raised, awaited the orches- 's supple return. The harmony. Fingers trembling slightly, bare- higher than the piano itself: perhaps slipping through waves real ough to touch, suspended on the silence of a clouded river, tween life and death . . .

These thoughts were Montserrat's, as she sat next to her hus- nd Miguel, in the Parisian concert hall on May 3, as the seconds ked monstrously by.

esday — Bourges

Montserrat, I lost you at Bourges, Bourges the incandescent.

Like that morning of December 31, 1506, Montserrat.

(Who knows what century or month we were in, Montserrat . . . I'm not e of a thing, except you, when an embrace leaves you speechless, riveted ne. Then, at last, you abide.)

When the North Tower crumbled,

Dragging down vault and portal,

Then I thought of you, my one and only love of
precious moment, forever evanescent. I was workin
Beethoven concerto (the Fourth), and can still hea
me, with an echo of you. Oh, how I wish I were you
to translate the overpowering emotion of music!

What did you do today, Montserrat? Although yo
like the freest person on earth, I'm afraid you migh
gentle slave. That is why I could never be an obstac
innocent love of life and death. Love death, Montse
it cannot hurt you. *(It holds Miguel's dark happiness.)*

Do you remember Rondo Vivace? It's built like a
don't you think? The precise voice of the orchestra
the silence of each stone, the sleeping dismay of ea
with a bright halo . . . and suddenly, I saw Montserr
through the fog, and then I lost her.

(The stone, the silence of each stone, is my hand raised
piano . . . I expect tragic powerlessness, but I must wait s
Then the violent cry of the instruments returns suddenly:
song, modest as a child's voice, and I understand, in an
plenitude, that at last my hands have dared rejoin the su

Montserrat. Montserrat.

I saw a multitude of stained-glass windows, all refl
grey of your eyes, and from those darkened panes e
as if summoned, a shading between reflection and l
pillars of the vault had infinite depth and height . .
to lose you. Oh, Montserrat . . .

Confessors and extravagant prophets, forever imp
their cathedral of dream, for an instant saw the pass
shadow . . .

Suddenly, a tomb, and I saw your hand resting on
inconsolable.

Oh, Montserrat.

Thus you were in my heart, all through the Rond
I understood that you'd already bid me goodbye.

The whole cathedral fell,

Dragging down your body and mine,

And for hours we were asunder.

"Tell me what you were thinking, Miguel. I know: in the mid-sixteenth century, there were five covered portals and countless sculptures . . . trees full of birds. First, there . . ."

Miguel looked at her, never having seen her in this way before. Yes, keep on talking, Montserrat. She felt troubled, covering her eyes with the back of her right hand: sheltered thus from an imperceptible hurt, she thought about him and saw his dark lashes shining.

"First, leaning against the eighth pillar of the nave, there were sculptures representing scenes of the Passion, and enclosing the choir . . ."

"No," said Miguel, "that wasn't it."

". . . and the angels, and six copper columns."

"You don't believe a word of this," said Miguel.

Then I said to him, "Tell me which you have chosen, me or the flames."

For the flames came from the gardens

Great and glorious flowers, you were witness to the Last Judgement

Great and glorious flowers, you last as long as a word

Why the fire, Miguel?

"No, no, that isn't what I was thinking," said Montserrat.

Then I said, "Tell me which you have chosen."

You, my love. You knew that already.

Don't leave me, then.

Only to find you again . . . I have to.

I'll be swept away like a wave. I feel myself slipping into the conflagration of stones.

The pillars come crashing down, and I see myself tangled in their tracings of fire.

The flames or me,

See,
You, Miguel, you
Where go the smoke-filled chapels?
Where go the windows, deeply wounded?
Where goes Montserrat, torn?
With you
Eastward
A cathedral kneeling in ash
For those days and nights, we were separated.
"You, Miguel. I've told you already. You."

Montserrat looked at him. Petrified in front of one another in the doorway of the cathedral at Bourges, they spoke softly. The woman saw the man was weeping.

I lay down next to her on the copper tomb, and we waited for night.

Tuesday night

DEAR JOHANN,

I beg of you . . . quit Montserrat's life, and mine. You have no idea of the danger you pose for us. It is a bewitching illusion of paradise, as full of risk as any there can be. "Yes, we must keep him at a distance." We sought spiritual escape in the cathedrals of France. *(After all, it was a kind of spell you'd put on us.)* We went on a voyage to recover our souls, and do you know what we found? You, Johann, you were present everywhere and in everything — cheated at every turn!

Tomorrow is Wednesday: leave at dawn, please. My wife and I wish to have a few days of peace before your triumph in Venice on Sunday. Before you came into our existence, we were in love with one another, and thus with life itself.

We never thought about death. She loved me, and I loved her. Our happiness arose from perfect harmony and from the fact that I was enough for her, and she for me. We wanted for nothing as we journeyed through our days. Our decline was a pristine one. We were satisfied, if not ecstatic. Then, suddenly, Montserrat discovered a sublime temptation in you that I do not understand — and I, too, though at another level, I believe. She was taken by thirst, and I by hunger. We grew apart and became frightened. At Chartres and at Bourges, on a tomb of bronze or copper or stone, we desired and rediscovered our estranged bodies, moaning over our disparate limbs. You see, you inspired a soul so grand and wild in us that we ended up brutalizing all our desires.

Perhaps you belong to the race of the Immortals *(like those magnificent angels I saw at Chartres . . . that is, other than Montserrat leaning her head on my shoulder),* and that immortality is the temptation you have brought us . . . your words, your voice too pure and piercing, but we won't succumb. We would rather live and die, or die ceaselessly, never to be reborn. We made that decision as children, she and I, one hot day in Madrid, when first I discovered the pink of her shoulder . . .

I realized that on Sunday, as the curtain came down on the last act of my play. It was an admirable, melancholy twilight, a twilight of emptiness. She's afraid of anything from the past that might come back to life. She's afraid of seeing me appear through her. That's the way Montserrat is. Sometimes I wonder why her eyes are so beautiful at day's end, and I realize they are the two quiet ghosts of what is not and what never has been, of all that has known the pain of not being. She is mortal . . . like me.

We are strangers, you and I, even though we are subject to the same law of creation. Everything you create is struck with immortality, but for Montserrat and me, everything crumbles in our hands from the moment we give it form. I know what you are thinking.

From sketches and magic, you've seen Montserrat bring forth a splendid male forehead, or the triumphant look of a young woman, or the darkened, down-turned mouth of a child. Well, these sculptures were only passing visitors to earth: at the very hour and second I am writing this, they are already in the process of self-destructing, just like anything else made by man. Whatever we are perishes minute by minute. We have no idols but the cult of our love for one another, though it is not an ecstatic cult. It is more level than the desert. I have no complaint about how we are, but please, you must leave us what is ours, what always has been ours through the centuries. If there is no future life waiting for us, we have at least what was — the secrets, links to our lives of now.

Montserrat hasn't a clue what she is doing: she sees you as a diabolical presence, but so strong a temptation could only be an angel . . . something that has always frightened me more than the Devil himself. His is the persecution I fear.

Remember the first time we met. Montserrat was curled up and smiling in a shadowy corner of the apartment, languishing at the sound of your voice.

"Miguel, recite a poem for us, darling . . ."

The suppleness of her voice, the poise of her body, sudden, unexpected, along the wall, leaping out of the shadows to get a better look at you. It was the Devil she saw. The unknowing-ness in her face told me that.

"Come on, Miguel!"

> Once, only once,
> I want to see the spirit
> Of this body lying beside me,
> Take it at last, like a wounded sun,
> In an irreversible embrace
> And its own space . . .

Listen . . . she goes on, once again inert before you . . .
Listen:

> Breath of autumn on my solitary brow
> You know not whom I love,

You know not where I live.
Your long eyes of snow
Lead me nowhere.
You know not whom I mourn, .
Nor of whom I sing.
If you were not, O senseless Earth,
I would seek for you in God . . .
Breath of autumn on my solitary brow
I plunge at last to the roots of fire!
Hopeless, from wind-to-wind I went
Shaken by the heavenly hurricane
Hopeless, from wind-to-wind I went
Weep, oh weep, you living one!
I have veiled the soul, too naked,
Of this body that lies beside me . . .

"Be quiet," I told Montserrat, and she was — though still
rebellious, she continued to wait for something. Finally, she
spoke. *(Chilled and sad, I had withdrawn to have a better look
at Paris in the rain; I wanted to hear you laughing together and
discover an angel's laugh in the embarrassed laughter of my wife.
It was not to be, just these few words of Montserrat's, perhaps . . .)*

"Yes, I too am moved at the thought of his writing, but
Johann . . . *(No, she repeats your name with desperation.)* Johann, my
friend doesn't know what he's saying, doesn't know that all this is
really very little, nor how nor why he's inspired to these lines, nor
by whom . . . and I don't want him to know: he's simply writing
about his mortal state — he writes with ashes, and we live with
blood *(she needed to feel her heart beating, like a young girl deep in
thought, one hand on her breast).* Johann, oh Johann, how he's going
to suffer tomorrow! *(Her heartbeat becomes irregular, and she instantly
resembles the old woman she'll never have time to be!)* Let's keep suffering far away from us, Johann! My husband writes so many words
without realizing the weight they carry. Even as a small boy, he

wrote about the deaths of bulls in his notebooks at school. That's where I first saw blood spilled . . . leaning over him, while he traced huge red letters with his black pen. I watched a wound open, and then I forgot. I was with him in Rome, at that university — I forget the name; he remembers everything about our past, but I don't — while he went on writing appalling words in the great, unknown vengeance of war. He could write about the song of fountains, too, though, and the lament of the sleep-bound . . . so many things long gone!

"I've seen this wild adolescent before, prowling the streets of Rome . . ."

The wind rippled Montserrat's hair. *(At that moment, I came back and closed all the doors.)* I leaned over the warm nape of her neck, but only in thought.

"Miguel, how cool it is suddenly!"

You were there . . . you were always there, spying on me without knowing it.

Wednesday: the cathedral at Reims

MIGUEL, MIGUEL, RECITE that poem to me. It will remind me of you till the day I die. Perhaps, if you want me to, Miguel, I can remember you beyond death. That way, you would be my immortality, and I would need no other.

Yes, I want your body never to forget the smallest part of my soul.

Miguel, Miguel, when my mother was dying alone and without God, we asked her, "Who do you want to see? Who do you want to love? Eternity is near . . . this is the last instant. Soon, it will all be over. You must open your eyes to that which has no end." And do you know what she answered?

"May my body never forget the smallest part of my soul."

"My mother was very young when she died," said Montserrat. "Nobody knew that as well as I did."

"Where is my lover? Where is my husband?" said my mother.

So my father came closer and held her hand.

"Montserrat," he said, "I can no longer exist in the face of God."

"Be quiet," said Miguel.

He placed his hand over Montserrat's mouth and held it shut. "Be quiet," he begged with fierce sweetness. Then he took away his hand, and Montserrat looked at him, her eyes watchful in the silence of night.

"Sometimes, Miguel, you confuse my far-off thoughts with what you think you hear me say."

"Yes," he said humbly.

"Sometimes, Miguel, you confuse what you think with what you write."

"Yes."

"About that poem, please recite it to me one last time, and tell me what you saw in the cathedral at Reims."

"I believe I said a prayer," he replied.

Montserrat pursed her lips in an effort to concentrate.

> In the cathedral at Reims,
> On this May morning,
> A king was crowned
> See the chevet Angel pass . . .
> See the chevet Angel . . .

"It is 1328, and the coronation of Philippe VI is about to take place . . . The king I'm talking about knows nothing of his power. The king I'm talking about is just a child. There is no time for him. See the chevet Angel pass . . .

> In the cathedral at Reims,
> On this May morning,
> A child was sacrificed."

No, Miguel, no . . . you know it happened only in your mind. We had barely stepped through the portal, when a crowd of kids came toward us. Like a field of lilies spread out across the horizon, these were the first communicants of the month of May.

I said to him, "Miguel, stay with me," but he let himself be swept away by this flurry of pure wings. He drowned at the centre of my soul.

Miguel, Miguel.

In the cathedral at Reims that I contemplated like a century lost, I saw before me the awesome unity and the singing city of symmetry —

Among all these gigantic proportions, I saw the passions of men, like luminous winds,

Harmony was sculpted into the features of the chevet Angel,

O brutal wind, O tender wind

Blowing past the winds of Judgement Day.

"No, my darling," said Montserrat, "You know perfectly well it was all in your mind."

"Perhaps it was," he said.

I said to him, "Miguel, don't leave me."

The cathedral towered over the town,

And over the world,

Miguel, I am simply someone who loves all that.

You shouldn't leave me.

The Gallery of the Prophets . . .

It's as though God's thinking . . . look, Miguel

No, Montserrat, it's the bright delirium of your mind.

A row of white slabs bordered by black stones

The children walk, and their shadows fly

Is it a dream, Miguel?

Everything was a dream to you, Montserrat.

Montserrat's mind is a valley flowering in joyful disorder.

But these mazes, I'm sure I saw them, Montserrat

And those high vaults, arching into the transparency of sky

Miguel, Miguel, you were in exile. You saw nothing.

And the six towers . . . the seven stairs of black marble

The columns, slender as paddle blades

And that rose, Miguel, that rose of six petals
Opening to the west.
It has since closed. Your eye perceives only beauty.
"Recite the poem to me," begged Montserrat.
"Yes," Miguel said.
The man's voice, in a solitary cascade of lament, burned the blood.
Andantino. The woman's memory burned his blood.

> In the cathedral at Reims,
> On this May morning,
> The melancholy child fell silent
> Receiving the crown of thorns
> In the cathedral at Reims,
> "Say nothing to his mother
> Far off at home, weaving.
> Say nothing to his mother."
> Thus the first red snow of blood
> Ran down the child's brow.
> Say nothing to his mother,
> Far off at home, weaving
> For her son.
> For the child will die today
> In the cathedral at Reims.
> He is the sacrificial prince
> Each day, a child dies
> In a cathedral.
> Each day, dew kills the carnation
> So that you may live, Montserrat.
> Each hour, the child disappears
> In the foam of oceans
> So that you may live, Miguel.
> I weave the tunic of pearls
> He must wear tomorrow.

Say nothing to his mother,
Sewing the fragile funeral clothes,
So that you may love, Montserrat.
Thus the warm south of his blood
Falls onto the child's fingers
And generous, stricken hands
Lay necklaces of thorns.
O Briers, you weep
When the thoughtful child,
Beneath heavy lids, dares not murmur.
Thus the first mourning for his blood
Falls onto the child's fingers.
I weave the tunic of silk
My son must soil tomorrow.
Say nothing, no, nothing, to his mother.
What has become of the nightingale
In our house?
Messenger of the moon,
Couldn't he come to me?
What has become of the forgotten
Nightingale . . .
Couldn't he share my wound?
I die for one who does not know me yet.
Each hour, a child
Becomes captive to unfinished redemption.
What has become of the nightingale
In our house?
Couldn't he come to me?
Crucify him . . .
Who said that?
You or I, Montserrat
You or I, Miguel
On this May morning

The child stripped of his clothes
(Then, his mother, leaning over the tunic she has been sewing, sees a drop of blood appear, like a tear in the hollow of a feeling mirror.)
Trembling on the verge of grace
And nakedness,
The child is abandoned at noon
Burst with suffering
Say nothing to his mother.
She thinks he is dazzled
By the mirage of Jerusalem's fountains.
(Now, already, she is forgetting the drop of blood.)
The child is crucified
In the cathedral at Reims.
Nailed feet and hands,
The child is crucified
In the cathedral of France,
And finally on his bleeding side
Spread the first snows
Of death.
(Now, already, she is forgetting the death of her child.)

Montserrat opened her eyes. The voice of the man fell silent. "Darling," she said, "this 'Poem of the Passion' never existed, except in your mind."

"Perhaps," Miguel said.

"It was merely a dream. I'm frightened," said Montserrat. "Because it might be true, too."

She remembered the end of that day in Reims. She had found Miguel again. She had knelt before him and said, "I'm afraid of loving you too much." He had caressed her nape, which gently met his hand. "Miguel, do you hear me? I'm afraid of taking up all that space in you — what should I call it? — the forbidden place, God's portion."

"It doesn't matter," said Miguel.

He repeated those same words in the train, on the way back to Paris, without any anxiety.

"You don't really weigh what I say to you, do you Miguel?"

"Montserrat, don't be afraid. I know what I want."

Suddenly, some young people came into the compartment. Miguel looked away, like a man weary of himself. Montserrat recognized the young pianist and her fiancé John, as well as the children who had been singing in the cathedral all day.

"You remember us, don't you? This is Miguel, and I'm Montserrat. Were you in Reims today?"

"Yes," said the girl. "My fiancé set a poem to music in the cathedral."

She asked Miguel, "Where are you from?"

"I wish I knew," was his reply.

SECOND INSTANT

"What country is it? I do not
know. There, things correspond.
They melt gently into one another.
I know it exists somewhere. I can
even see it, but I do not know
where it is, and I cannot go there."
                    — Kafka

"YOUR FACE BELONGS to me, and yet I do not know it. It is Thursday."

Allegro Ma Non Troppo.

On this May Sunday in Paris, at the beginning of the third movement, Montserrat felt her heart weaken, and suddenly, her face clouded, savouring the beginnings of a delicate and vaporous dizziness. She had always felt close to all living things, and with that same wholeness of heart that resisted the tumult of her blood. She had formed herself to its regular certainty, as she had to Miguel's heart and to the inexhaustible vastness of his being.

"My heart is too slow. You are so slow."

"What did you say?" asked Miguel. "What's wrong?"

In his empty profile, she saw her own face absorbed, reflected. Thus, Miguel found himself placing his hand on his own heart and thinking, My blood is leaving me. I shall die soon.

"Be quiet, dear," he said.

Suddenly, Montserrat remembered the day and the moment when she had felt this same dull distress, this separation of body and soul *(just before complete separation)*. Yes, it was Thursday at eight o'clock, in the arms of Johann.

Allegro Ma Non Troppo.

The end of this movement would also bring the end of Montserrat. She knew that. Johann was playing with blessed simplicity. What he knew, and what he did not know, of this contemplative movement blended in him, in the humble power of his hands; he was the eagle and its prey, the found and the lost.

Allegro Ma Non Troppo.

These thoughts were Montserrat's, as she sat next to her husband.

Montserrat, still thrilling from the week she had lived through, struck forever with a revelation greater than anything she could fathom.

"Yes, Thursday . . . that face."

Thursday

"What have you done with Miguel?"

"He's walking down by the docks."

"In this rain?"

"Yes, in this rain."

He took Montserrat's hands, unfolded them on the bedside table, in the direct light of the lamp. "There are countless wounds here. Why?"

"I've been cutting clothes for Miguel all day. You can see lines from the needles." She laughed.

"Why ruin your hands?"

"My hands, poor Johann, all they're good for is tailoring capes for Miguel."

"What about your sculpture?" He pointed to the tall, immobile figures around them, crowding in, like ghosts of their obscure love.

"They aren't really mine," she said.

"Then where did they come from?"

"You know that better than my own soul does," Montserrat answered. "Don't ask me any questions."

The next three days ran parallel to the first three. Monday, Tuesday and Wednesday had seen the storm and the pursuits through the cathedrals of France — now came three days of ship-wreck. The remaining time was indifferent to this sudden down-pour. Montserrat had known three days of despair, and — in the immensity of days over the unquiet earth — she could manage three more that were all too short . . . days which would give hope to her flesh before its final dissolution. At last, Johann had arrived to share this diabolical hope, and she wanted nothing more . . . one thing, perhaps — not to forget Miguel, to be at his service until he died . . . and to love him more than herself, when he was reduced to those few ashes she already saw at the end of his life, a handful of ashes rustling in her hand.

"First, a woman doesn't harm her own hands and mouth . . ."

"I don't know how we die," replied Montserrat cruelly.

"Where are you, Montserrat, where . . . so faithless and faithful, all at the same time?"

"I know where we are, Johann: in the middle of a downpour in Paris. Other houses are swallowed up, but ours remains. Yes, I know all that. I have for a long time. I'm lying, Johann. You're what interests me . . . your secret, and you won't tell it, even in your sleep. This body of yours . . . do you think that's enough for me? No, I sense only too well what it conceals. When I was hungry as a child and they gave me bread, that didn't assuage my hunger for the supernatural. It's the same with you. You are an angel or a demon, and if neither one, then nothing."

"I'm a man," he said. "Don't persist in believing anything else."

(More gently, enclosing Montserrat's hands in his, as one might cover a surface too sensitive to any sort of contact.)

"Montserrat, I also want to know who you are!"

"Well then, Johann, what would you like to know? Yes, it's true I've lived only for him . . . and so what? Is there anything besides death for one who has loved so much? Protect him. Don't tempt him with that strange immortality. I feel him tempted, wanting to leave me, to go further on in time. *(Love . . . isn't it the god of wasted time?)* That's all I can be to him . . . all. What have you done to him? Why have you come? I remember, as a child, wanting to know you . . . to see your eyes . . . to be taken by you. Oh yes, I wanted that, but why? Absurd, wasn't it? Your contented peacefulness sits in judgement on us."

"Montserrat, I believe you are afraid of your body's reaching an end, because you're convinced there can't be a new beginning afterwards."

"None at all. Take me again, and show me for an instant, a brief instant, whether it's within our power *(the Devil's beauty is all-powerful)* that intimate eternity which will soon be taken from me."

"No," said Johann. "Keep far away from me."

Montserrat entered the embrace as if it were a tomb, eyes shut, seeing her limbs stretched out far beyond her, long and thunderstruck, savouring the relaxation in its immensity, becoming little by little the rising plain, immobile one moment and raised the next, freed by winds of pleasure, and again banished to modesty. Then, suddenly, the cloud-happiness of sleep seized her; one by one, her fingers — half-opened roses — closed. Imperceptibly, her fair stomach, like a bird caught up in dizziness, darkened and refused any trembling caress, as golden corn hides from the burning sun.

Neck and shoulders allowed themselves to float into a delicious void, like a tree that tumbles majestically in a great green silence that is foreign to the silence of distress. Montserrat's shoulders and breasts were to her as the tragic bark to the tree *(rapid and changing, they could be seen separating from the tree, stretching and hiding themselves)* while her blood remained its lifeblood, the original sacred river, and her legs stretched out, the rich sacrifice in a black crucible.

Montserrat slept embraced in the heart of a grave, in the heart of a tree. She dared not violate with a cry the mourning formed around her by the the thin forest of the world.

When she awoke, she felt the growing wounds of love. The instant was already one more past. Johann, lying beside her, feigned silence, his body seemingly placed across the absent body from which he had just separated, with the true cruelty of remembrance.

"Johann, Johann," Montserrat murmured.

But he must not have heard her. She was alone, and her heart beat slowly. How could she call it back to life and warmth? "You're leaving me, leaving me. Living heart, you are all I have."

Sitting next to the man, Montserrat knew she had been torn from his side, and she let him sleep, for she knew that she had always been the wound in his sleep.

"Johann, Johann, you reign over these bones
And I over your blood.
We are one
Beyond our wills
Without lasting . . ."

Perhaps the woman, leaning over his pale side, as over a diaphanous river, discovered the secret of a thin-channelled suffering that was born with her. She wanted only to prevent herself from screening that mysterious estrangement she found too sweet, alienation from Man's suffering.

"Now," she thought, "I can embrace Miguel and breed this strength in him, this luminosity that I feel deep in myself, or rather these absolute and blinding shadows."

"Johann, listen to me!"

He opened his eyes and lamented his pent-up body: "Montserrat, who has removed a piece of my flesh?"

"I have," she said, "while you slept."

"You knew it would harm me," said Johann.

"Yes, I knew."

Towards the end of the evening, Montserrat was sculpting Johann's face. The oncoming cool of night combined with the fatigue in her fingers, and Montserrat was able to create a man.

"What's wrong, Montserrat?"

"Nothing, Johann, but this is my last creation, and it will cost me my life. Why are you so disturbed? As you live off me, so by degrees I die. I still must leave you my expression . . . I must . . ."

"Oh, do be still," he begged. "You are so weary, love."

The light had gone out of Montserrat's eyes and left behind no tears.

"Yes, I am very tired," the woman said.

Thursday night

Miguel! Miguel!

Montserrat had waited for him on every doorstep in Paris. She had run to the docks. She had watched for him at the Métro exit. He was gone, still in panic-stricken flight, the same that had led him to Bourges, seeking to keep within him the majestic cry from Paris.

"Miguel!"

All at once, she saw him, alone and panting for breath. She took his arm and got him to follow her home. The rain was beginning to freeze on the streets.

"You are so cold, Miguel. We'll make a nice fire in the room."

She smiled as she always had, as she had on Monday, coming back from Chartres.

"If only you knew how much I've hungered to take you in my arms," said Miguel.

"Were you looking for the angel?"

"No, running away from it."

". . . and tomorrow, Miguel?"

"I'll run from it again, and you?"

"I've found what I was looking for, and I want to get so close I'll never be away from it again."

". . . and tomorrow, Montserrat?"

"I'll do it again," she said.

They were standing before the five metal steps between them and their apartment, the locked doors to their rooms.

"We'll never make it," she said.

Then, triumphant, Miguel took his wife in his arms and climbed each step, supporting his light prey, whose eyes never left him, and who sank into his shoulder, grateful and faithful in this secret wedding.

Montserrat leaned toward the fire that warmed the entire room and rubbed her hands, watchful of Miguel.

"What have you done to your hands and eyes, Montserrat?"

"Every day you'll ask me that, won't you, Miguel? I shall age with passion. Don't worry about me. Am I so ugly since I started dying?"

"No," he said.

"Hold me up with those huge hands of yours. Yes, I'm going to die."

Her words had stirred him to pity.

And from this further embrace, he arose with a wound to the heart.

Spain in dream

"You were ten years old, Montserrat, or maybe it was eight,
When first I saw you in a church in Barcelona.
'Keep her far away from me,' I told my mother and sisters
'She is too beautiful for me to like
She is too sweet for me to love'
But already I knew she would be waiting
For me, the world over . . .
With that same fatal smile."
"Tell me why the Virgin is busy spinning
When the angel's message comes . . .
Tell me why."
I didn't say anything, Montserrat.
You were nine years old, Montserrat, or maybe it was thirteen.
When you came to me during that pilgrimage to the Virgin
It was a night lit up by Montserrat.
And I put my arm around your waist:
"Pray with me, Montserrat, pray with me."
I did not pray
I saw Miguel in a garden in Barcelona
At evening, we slept on a boat
In the middle of the sea
And at each dawn we awoke
In the Bay of Palma in Majorca,
The silver coast faded
To the port, and far off, like a mountain
The cathedral . . .
"What church was that in Barcelona?"
"Santa Maria del Piña."
"No," Miguel said, "It was Santa Maria del Mar. It was in May."
"Tell me why the Virgin is busy spinning
When the angel's message comes . . .

Tell me why," but he said nothing.
My mother's face was veiled in black,
"Keep away from me, Miguel. Walk with your sisters."
We were headed for Avila
My mother's hands were veiled in blue
My sisters wore skirts as deep as the sky
On them were embroidered stars and flowers
I loved the narrow trace of their agile waists
We were headed for Avila
On the way, tired old women
Leaned their heads against the setting sun,
Calmly breathing
"Miguel, Miguel, why are you crying?"
A brown and faithful beacon
Our little donkey gazed longingly
At every well along the way
You were ten years old, Montserrat, or maybe it was seven,
When I saw you walk towards me, erect and splendid
Eyes closed, toward an innocent executioner
Not knowing he would tie you forever to that setting sun
In Avila
As to the bleeding passion of his heart.
"There, the mountains stood up straight as thorn-bushes
Sad olive-trees curved beneath the winds"
"No," said Miguel, "only the olive-trees stood straight up
In Spartan solitude,
Unexpected as a sad note on a harp . . ."
"Tell me why the Virgin is busy spinning
When the angel's message comes."
"Far, very far away, in that church in Barcelona
I said nothing, Montserrat."
Take me to Madrid
Keep far away from me
Am I not your fiancé?

Take me to Madrid
You're not even fifteen
Madrid, the Church of San José,
"Tell me why the Virgin is busy spinning
When the angel's message comes."
In the Plaza Monumental, is it
The running of the bulls or the running of the stars?
Miguel could think of nothing but me,
And I of nothing but him.
Between us but one distance,
The beating of a fan,
"Get rid of that fan. It's hiding your eyes."
I didn't listen, the better to concentrate on him
"Cruel woman, what have you done!"
I wanted him to realize that other distance
Which will always be there.
"Did you understand that, Miguel?"
"No, only later, much later."
"You're giving me a fever, Montserrat. Please listen."
To others, we seem as one
God made us inseparable,
As much for one as for the other
"Infinite distance, Montserrat."
That sole distance was enough to split the world
"Lower that fan . . . a thirst is rising in me. I must see you."
Fire and shadow, as she raised and lowered it
Never did I know the repose in her eyes,
The running of the bulls or the running of the stars?
The *alquazils* rode past, the *picadors*
and the *banderillos*
All preparing the festival of agony
And I had only Montserrat
To give me a thousand deaths,
Ceaseless lover for a lifetime . . .

The mounted *picadors* first pierced
Their victim, weakened, barely rebelling
I suffer . . . bleeding, I suffer
No, Montserrat, no
The *banderillos* torture him next
Approaching, barely touching in insidious torment
"Among the oppressed, you are oppressed; with the strong, you
rise again."
"Yes," Miguel said,
"No, now listen to me, Montserrat . . . your eyes . . ."
It is the final stroke, and the *matador* awaits his triumph
Burning fingers drop her fan
Why are you crying, Miguel?
"That infinite distance . . . at last I understand it."

LAST INSTANT
Friday: Paris in dream

FROM ÎLE SAINT-LOUIS, they could see the chevet of Notre-Dame,
a perfect union of glistening stone. Montserrat's voice approached
Miguel's cheek, then vanished at once, brutal and swift as swan-
flight in the night.

"No, Miguel, you still don't understand this infinite distance,
no, not at all."

"Then you've heard me speak to you in dreams?"

"Yes."

"Don't feel hurt, Montserrat. It was just a dream of a dream."

"I heard everything."

"Gently, Montserrat."

"Do you remember Grenada, when everything kept us apart . . .
the colours of sky and water, the word of a child in the house, the
look of a strange woman — forgive me, but I feel it again, this split.
I don't know where it's coming from."

Rain spread from time to time on Miguel's forehead, like the

balm of snow. "I'm not in pain," he said. "I feel nothing any more."
I don't know what it means to be "separated from someone we
love." Why would we do that? We're together.

"I know it was very humiliating for you at dress rehearsal on
Sunday, Miguel."

"It's forgotten now," he said.

". . . humiliating, too, to know that Johann would never understand you."

"Perhaps," he said, "but I've really forgotten all of it so I can
think only about you."

On Sundays, at the horse races,
I went and sat next to him in the gardens
Alone under a huge, full moon
Watching the mysterious ride
Running straight — beautiful, pale, tawny horses
Melting into golden corn
Miguel Miguel
White horses running
Over the frozen river

"What are you doing?" Miguel asked. "Yes, why hide your face
behind your umbrella? You know how much I need to look at you."

On Sundays, at the horse races
I went and sat next to him in the gardens at Saragossa.
Our parents said,
"Let's leave these children of tragedy in peace
They belong together
Throughout the centuries."
"Fire and shadow . . . never can I know the repose of your eyes."
The running of horses or the running of the stars
With such a delicate hand I mounted his horse
He took hold of me to feel I was his,
And yet, when he opened his hands,
It was enough to lose me
Montserrat, Montserrat, he said, and I brought my lips close to

his mouth
Miguel, Miguel, I said
You are a Levantine fisherman
And he laughed
The running of horses or the running of the stars
I no longer sat next to him
On Sundays in Saragossa, for we'd grown up
And were people of the universe.
And like his laughter, the autumn wind
Flowed from branch to branch.
"I must see you," Miguel begged.
The umbrella fell from Montserrat's burning fingers
"It's nothing, Miguel, nothing. I'm here."
And she heard him laugh . . . as he used to.

Friday. Night-time.

MONTSERRAT, HER ARMS hanging by her sides, like a boat pushing back foam-topped waves, glided from silence to silence, till she reached that abyss of astonished unconsciousness where she opened her eyes from time to time, in order to remind herself, cautiously, that Miguel still existed.

"Why spend so much time sewing, Montserrat? You have so many years stored up, still."

"And you, Miguel, what is it you want to do? You know full well that temptations do not die away."

Miguel drew the curtains and saw the works of night-time, the barren statues born of Montserrat's lively mind, radiating their gilded, secret warmth to the peace that was in his eye. At length, their warmth pervaded his body and soul; he felt the sudden, dark stirring of a thought that tied him to all his wife created . . . and he was moved.

"What do you want to do, Miguel?"

Montserrat's beseeching was like a fearful lament; it touched and irritated the violence in him.

"Why kill your brother, Cain? Don't you hear God's distress?"

Suddenly, these statues, which had been like lifelong sisters to him, and children to Montserrat (perfect obedience in every character's face) no longer held that supreme submission to Miguel's will: suddenly, they were turning against him. Inexplicable and hostile, Miguel saw them closing in on him. One of them was destroying all the others. One of them . . . Johann.

"What are you doing, Miguel? What is it you want to do?"

Oh Miguel, how sad in victory . . . kneeling before broken bits of a statue! Miguel, Miguel!

Night had fallen. Montserrat heard the rattle of rain on the Paris rooftops. Such was the echo within her that she felt revived. She got up and dropped her arm to her side: "How wonderful I feel!"

"I'm sorry, darling," said Miguel, "I'll repair everything."

"No, Miguel, there's no need. I like them better as relics. Look . . . rose-petals."

"A flower," he agreed.

"Our springtime's nearly over," she said. She felt unfathomable sadness at finding herself so much like him, already consumed in his approaching ashes.

Saturday
allegro ma non troppo.

"TOMORROW'S SUNDAY, Johann, isn't it? Why haven't you left already?"

"Tomorrow, I play," said Johann. "You know how serious it all is to me. I've been working to prepare this concerto properly for months."

"For years," the woman sighed, shrugging.

Pressed to the wall, Montserrat listened to him. She brought to mind the debris of their strange adventure, dimly searching for the compelling, sensual exaltation that had thrown her — both the purest and impurest of things together — into his arms. "Do what you will with me," she said.

"That's monstrous. Take it back."

"I can't," she said, bridling.

He had already ceased to be the man she had held on the threshold of eternity. Johann's soul had saved his body. His radiant and sensitive soul . . .

"I won't," she said.

allegro ma non troppo.

THE MAN CONTINUED playing. Now something nameless burned in his eyes. What vibrated in his soul no longer had that furious resonance or calm which yesterday had overwhelmed Montserrat's memory. Everything was crumbling.

Johann had felt struck down by the arm of Miguel: "Will you remember me in Vienna?"

"Yes," he replied.

". . . and tomorrow in the eternal city, Venice?"

"Yes, Montserrat."

"What a liar you are! You've already forgotten the embrace that tells a woman she is predestined to a man, to his body and desire. You've forgotten our embrace in Paris, standing in the rain that night in May, and how the entire form of your body took hold of me by surprise, in astonishment and pleasure, at last taking me, upright and motionless, your hand on the back of my neck . . . and I looked at you closer and more gently. You've forgotten, Johann, and quickly I ran back to Miguel in our room and held him close, in the same way, and then I understood all over again. Miguel smiled and placed his hand on my neck and I closed my eyes."

allegro ma non troppo.

"COME CLOSER, MONTSERRAT." She obeyed. He placed his hand on her breast and closed his eyes: "This heart, poor heart . . ."

At the Place de l'Opéra, Miguel saw all around him, the immense azure . . . torn. He had found himself tottering like this before — shaken and staggering, transported before the miraculous breadth of the Mediterranean.

Montserrat. Montserrat.

He would wait here for her. Perhaps she would come, perhaps never. The first time he had seen her, he had felt a desire for the Mediterranean, and then a desire for her eyes, and peace came upon him. Montserrat had won him with a mere gesture of her finger, the motion of her shoulder. Oh, if only he hadn't loved so much! How tired he felt!

"With this cloak, you'll never be cold, my love

You'll feel no more pain

You can go to the ends of the earth."

"How many days did you spend making this, Montserrat?"

"One day was enough."

He walked toward her invisible silhouette (yesterday, it was sketched in fire and eclipsed all the suns of Spain), Montserrat, ready to come to him, bursting out of nowhere, Montserrat and her sisterly step.

"Closer, Montserrat, please . . ."

Miguel enjoyed being the slave of the last day of the world.

The rain shivered down his desolate limbs.

He saw his heart was an open cup.

Blood ran down his clothes.

With this cloak, you'll feel no more pain, my love . . .

"Miguel, you weren't going to wait for me?"

With neither sadness nor strength, she stood there.

"Miguel, your heart . . . poor heart."

She placed her hand on his chest, closing her eyes.

His wound healed inside him.

allegro ma non troppo.

THUS WENT THE END of the last movement. Johann stood up. His hour of triumph burst like an indescribable rumble through the Paris concert hall on this Sunday, the third of May.

Montserrat willed herself to turn back to Miguel, but he was already gone.

Some time later, she went to Johann, who took her hands in his: "No, Montserrat, you must not wish to abandon it all."

"But I do want to," she said.

"And Miguel?"

"I'll find him."

He watched her go. He was thinking about many things at once. He was happy. They had just told him that his second child had been born. He hoped he'd be returning to Vienna soon . . . he hoped . . .

The Seine had already carried away Miguel, body and soul, alone in the grief of water. Running along the docks, Montserrat reached the edge, opened Miguel's tomb and lay down with him.

The Paris downpour ended.

The Place de l'Opéra was burnt in an instant. Montserrat would have perished there, the man she had loved never knowing.

In Vienna that day, it was snowing, and Johann's child was born.

ABOUT THE AUTHOR

Born in Québec City in 1939, Marie-Claire Blais has been a dominant figure in Canada's literary landscape for more than 40 years. At twenty, she published her first novel, *La Belle bête,* translated as *Mad Shadows.* In it, she analyzes with fierce lucidity the psychological motivations for a woman's hatred of her beautiful and simple-minded sister whom, in the novel's dénouement, she disfigures. While such violence and savagery are present in most of her novels and plays, they are never gratuitous, never complacent or exhibitionist. Her highly personal lyricism enables her to pass through the mirror of appearances and reveal hidden monstrosities. While still young, her talents were recognized by, among others, the American critic Edmund Wilson, who was instrumental in her receiving a Guggenheim Fellowship. *Une saison dans la vie d'Emmanuel* (Grasset, 1965) translated as *A Season in the Life of Emmanuel,* was awarded France's Prix Médicis and is now taught regularly in Canadian Studies courses. The impressive number of works that followed were produced at surprising speed. To date, some twenty novels have been published in France and in Québec, all of them translated into English. She is also a playwright, and in 1998 her collection of plays, *Wintersleep* appeared, published by Ronsdale Press. Marie-Claire Blais has spent extended periods of time in the United States, France, and China. Such recognition as the Canada-Belgium Prize in 1976, the France-Québec Prize and a number of grants have enabled her to devote herself to a work which is as authentic as it is striking and demanding. Her latest novel, *Soifs* (Boréal and Éditions du Seuil) translated as *These Festive Nights* (Anansi), received the Governor General's Award in 1997. Her short stories are as powerful as her novels, with all the added subtlety implicit in the shorter form. She is truly one of the outstanding chroniclers of our century.

ABOUT THE TRANSLATOR

Born in England and raised in London and Montréal, Nigel Spencer has also lived in Toronto and Guinea, West Africa. He now makes his home in Québec's Eastern Townships. He has studied literature, drama and education, principally at McGill and the University of Toronto. His work includes teaching, research, journalism, translation, film-subtitling and scripting, directing, acting, editing and writing. He is a co-founder of Toronto's Summer Centre Theatre and *Matrix* Magazine. He currently teaches Drama, Literature and African Studies at Champlain College in addition to translating works by Québec writers, including Marie-Claire Blais' *Wintersleep* (Ronsdale Press, 1998). Portions from a collection of his poems, titled "After-images," have been published in *Rampike* (Fall, 1998).